I0817884

PROTECTING THE INNOCENT

Nancy Powell

Book Two
The Keepers™ Series

TotalRecall Publications, Inc.
1103 Middlecreek, Friendswood, Texas 77546
281-992-3131 281

ISBN: 978-1-59095-505-5
UPC: 6-4397725056-8

Edited by: Jessica D. Caruso

Library of Congress Control Number: 2015954562

Printed in the United States of America with simultaneous printings in Australia, Canada, and United Kingdom.

FIRST EDITION

1 2 3 4 5 6 7 8 9 10

To my husband and best friend

About the Book

Anna heard the report of Jaeger's death, but she cannot believe it and continues to watch for him; he promised to hunt her down and kill her. Neighbor boys, Hank and Bill find themselves in trouble with the Game and Fish Commission, Child Services, and the Prosecuting Attorney, but the Dugans intercede and take the boys into their home as foster children. Also, they take a little girl whose parents were murdered—her biological father was wealthy, and she is first in line to inherit a fortune. Each child brings blessings and problems.

List of Main Characters

Anna Chapman – (POV) Red hair, brown eyes

Bart Grayson – (POV) Brown hair, blue eyes

Charles Dugan – Professor, brown hair, stocky build, a kind Christian man, Anna's boss

Mary Dugan – Slim, blond, beautiful, a compassionate Christian woman, Anna's boss

Carol Dugan – Blond hair, blue eyes, Charles and Mary Dugan's daughter

Jaeger – Anna's abductor, brown hair, brown eyes, muscular, 6'2"

Cara – Jaeger's mother

Jackie Freeman – Anna's friend, dark hair, brown eyes

Jason – Jackie's boyfriend

Danny – Foster child, the exterminator's grandson

Doug Miller – Detective, large man, he becomes a family friend

Hank – Neighbor boy, fourteen years old, Cherokee

Bill – Neighbor boy, six years old, Cherokee

Maddi – Girl from Carol's kindergarten class, black hair, smoky blue eyes

Joann – Hank and Bill's cousin

Curt – Hank and Bill's cousin, Joann's four-year-old son,

Mr. Prince – Appaloosa dealer, family friend

Polka – Anna's appaloosa horse

Apple – Carol's appaloosa horse

Curly – Family dog

About the Author

Nancy Powell has won several writing awards for short stories and poetry. Dark Secrets (under the name Ollie's Angels) won first place in the 2010 Mainstream Novel category at the Oklahoma Writers Federation, Inc. (OWFI) Contest. Also, the second book in the Ollie's Angels Series won an OWFI award in 2010. Dark Secrets was also awarded the 2012 third quarter Grand Prize at the "Books Without Publishers" writing contest sponsored at www.UltimateHeroContest.com.

Nancy Powell is married, the mother of two children, and has seven grandchildren. She is a member of the Church of Christ, River Valley Writers of Fort Smith, Oklahoma Writers' Federation, Inc., Greenwood Writers, and Round Table Poets.

In addition to writing, Nancy loves gardening, sewing, and painting. The paintings and book cover backgrounds in the Ollie's Angel Series are her interpretations in oil paint.

Acknowledgement

I want to thank my family for their love and support, and my writing friends for their help and encouragement.

Chapter 1

Exhausted from helping Bart work on the house where they will live after their wedding, Anna returns to the Dugan residence—her current home and workplace. She wolfs a piece of pie before remembering her counselor's advice to get a test for hypoglycemia, avoid sweets, and eat a high protein diet. Again, she looks in the refrigerator; everything high in protein requires cooking. Sleep is more important than food. She plods up the stairs. Eager to rest, she slips her loaded handgun underneath her bed. *I'll put it away in the morning.*

Downstairs, a pan clanks against the stove and silverware rattles. "Is it morning?" Anna slips into jeans as fast as she can, and grabs the door facing, to stop the room from turning. Blinking to clear the fog, she mumbles, "My blood sugar dropped."

Her blurred vision makes Anna forget the loaded gun. While working outside, the automatic weapon eases her fear of snakes, bears, and Jaeger, her abusive ex-husband. Jaeger was reported dead, but she cannot shake the feeling that he watches from the shadows, waiting to kill her.

Mary, Anna's employer, glances up from putting dishes in the dishwasher. "Good morning, Anna." Scrambled eggs and bacon are on the stove. Waffles are beside the toaster. "Danny and Bart ate with us and have gone already. Building a house is exhausting and requires food for energy." She smiles. "Danny should be okay 'til noon—he ate three servings."

"I didn't hear you or I would have helped cook breakfast."

"You needed the rest. You do more than your share of work for this family." She opens the pantry door. "I don't think I've ever let our grocery supply shrink this low. Charles and I are going shopping. We'll bring home burgers for lunch. Did you find something to eat last night?"

Anna nods. "The last piece of apple pie."

"That was a poor meal after you worked all day."

She shrugs. "I could have cooked, but I wanted sleep more than food. We accomplished a lot yesterday. Bart's rushing to get the house finished before the wedding."

Mary and Professor Dugan leave. Carol, their young daughter, sits on a stool, grinning and drumming fingers on the counter. Anna takes two bites of the egg before Carol asks, "How long until I get to ride my horse?"

"Did you pull the sheets off your bed? Remember, it's cleaning day."

"I forgot." The child runs up the stairs.

Anna downs a glass of orange juice and follows. "If you'll help dust and clean, I'll have time to give you another riding lesson."

"I already know how to ride."

"Do you think you know everything to be the best at barrel racing? What will you do if you are riding in the field and your horse steps on a sharp rock and goes lame? There's a lot more you need to know if you plan to become an expert with horses. I spent years learning."

Carol's shoulders slump. "All right, but can we hurry?"

Breakfast sits on the counter getting cold as Anna and Carol rush to change beds, dust, and vacuum. Glass shattering downstairs causes Anna to click off the vacuum. She whispers, "Get under my bed." Rushing to her closet, she reaches for a rifle kept on a high shelf, but Jaeger bounds up the stairs and grabs her arm before she can load it.

"You thought you were rid of me, didn't you, Red? I told you that I'd kill you if you ran away. You're going to suffer." Jaeger winds a hand in her long red hair and yanks her forward.

He blurs before her eyes. "The police said you were dead."

"Yeah, funny how they thought that big guy was me. I beat his face until no one could recognize him." He pushes her onto the twin bed, forcing it against the wall. Strands of her hair hang on his fingers like puppet strings.

Laughing, he leans over her. "Remember how I used to choke you until you blacked out? This time you won't wake up."

"No, Jaeg!" She kicks and slings her fists but is no match for his strength.

Twisting her hair with his left hand, he hits her face with his right. "Where's that kid you have tagging along everywhere you go?"

Anna does not answer—blood fills her mouth. Silently she prays, "Lord protect Carol."

Again, he pulls her forward, hits her, slams her onto the bed, grabs the front of her shirt and yells, "Where's the kid?"

Her ears ring and blood pours from her mouth. The coppery scent and taste causes her to gag.

He seems to be far away, yelling, "Tell me where you hid that kid?" With a curse, he lets go of her shirt, allowing her to fall across the bed and her head to bang against the wall.

Through a blur of blood and tears, she sees him bend to grab her and feels his big hands on her neck.

An explosion shakes the room, and her head hits the wall once more.

Hearing Carol calling her name, Anna tries to whisper, "Hush." The next thing she hears is a siren.

Carol gently washes Anna's face, and clings to her as men carry the gurney to an ambulance. A police officer tries to pull Carol away, but Anna grips her shirt, holding tight until she hears Mary's voice.

"Anna, it's all right. Jaeger is gone. I'll take care of Carol. They need to look at your eye."

Mary's words are clear as she gives instructions to someone in an unfamiliar room. "Call a plastic surgeon. I don't want this girl to have a scar. If you don't have one on duty, get one."

A warm sensation seeps through Anna's body.

* * * * *

In the dark room, Anna can only see shadows with one eye. She wants to touch a throbbing spot on her head, but cannot move her hands. She tries to call someone, but cannot open her mouth. She kicks—her feet are free. A blanket flies off the bed with a swish, but there are no other sounds in the room. She kicks her right foot as high as she can. A sharp pain runs through her foot, and something crashes to the floor.

A nurse runs in turning on lights and calling. "Anna, don't kick. Don't kick. Relax."

Bart stands beside the bed, his hair a mess, tears clouding his eyes. He rubs her arm. "Oh, Anna. I wish I'd been there to help you."

She wants to scream, "Tell me what happened." But she cannot open her mouth.

The nurse checks the IV. "We tied your hands to keep you from ripping out your IV. You were still trying to fight your attacker."

Anna groans and looks toward Bart. He tells her, "Jaeger is gone."

The nurse pats Anna's leg. "Hon, Mrs. Dugan got the best plastic surgeon in this area to work on your face. You won't have a trace of a scar."

She blinks her unbandaged eye and breathes deeply.

"We've restricted visitors. Today, only your family and fiancé can visit."

Anna slams her leg against the bed and does her best to frown at Bart.

"Jaeger's gone. Is that what you're wondering?"

She blinks, trying to see clearer. *Jaeg will come back—he always does.*

The nurse checks her blood pressure and temperature. "Your vitals are good, but I know you must be thirsty. The doctor said everything goes through the IV until tomorrow, and then maybe you can take liquids through a tube in your mouth. Sorry, that's doctor's orders."

The next time she wakes, the sunshine comes in the window behind Bart. Awake, with his hair combed, he sits rubbing her arm. "Anna, surely, your worst trials are over. I wish I could take you home to our little house and promise we'll live happy ever after."

She wants to hug and kiss him, but she can only blink one eye and worry. *Where is Jaeger? He'll come back to kill us.*

Bart rings for the nurse. "Can we take the restraints off her arms while she's awake? I'll hold her hands and call if she pulls at the IV."

The nurse looks at the IV port and pats her arm. "Honey, I'll release you if you'll promise to stay calm. Blink, if you understand what I'm saying."

Anna blinks, repeatedly.

The nurse laughs. "I know you want these off." She pulls at the tape and unwinds something.

Flexing and twisting her arms, Anna lifts her right hand and reaches to clasp Bart's warm fingers. After wringing their hands together, she motions as if writing. Bart gets a pencil and pad from the bedside stand.

She writes. "All along, I felt as if Jaeger was waiting to kill me, and he'll come back."

"No. He can't."

"He always does. Even if the police have him, he'll escape and be back."

"Anna, he's dead. You can relax. He's gone for good."

"I can't believe it unless I see him. Many times, Dad told him to leave our farm and never come back, but he continued to sneak around—watching me, or shooting and frightening our animals. Then within a week of Mom and Dad's funeral, Jaeger drugged me and arranged that mock wedding."

"Honey, he's gone this time—I'm sure of it. I saw him on a stretcher, white as a ghost."

"Are you positive? Did they take him to the hospital?"

"They took him to the morgue. He will *never* come after you again."

"Now, our lives can go forward?"

"Yes." He kisses her hand. "Was he the reason you were worried all the time?"

She blinks and writes. "I wanted my gun in my hand as I tried to look behind every tree for Jaeger. I was especially afraid when you kissed me—he was so jealous that I knew he'd kill us in a brutal way if he caught us together."

She rubs his hand again and picks up the pencil. "How bad is my eye? Does it have permanent damage?"

"It has a cut across the eyebrow and eyelid. There's no damage to the eye."

"How bad is my mouth? With my tongue, I don't feel any missing teeth."

"Your teeth are fine. You have a cut inside your top lip where he smashed it against your teeth, and cuts outside on the top and bottom lips from his fist. The plastic surgeon said you will be as beautiful as before and not have scars, but when he takes the bandages off, you should not touch your lips or eye. He taped uncut parts to keep your mouth closed."

She rubs the top of his hand before lifting the pencil again. "This will slow our house building."

"Danny and I will get that done, but the doctor said no kissing on the lips for a month. He doesn't want to take any chances on the cuts reopening."

She blinks twice. "A month is a long time. Was he kidding?"

"I don't think so. He looked serious."

She draws a sad face on the paper. "It felt as if Jaeger yanked out handfuls of my hair. Do I have bald spots?"

"I didn't notice any."

"Good. How is Carol? I hate that she was involved."

"She seemed calm—better than many adults would have

been. Danny and I heard the sirens and jumped in the truck. We got there soon after the police. He started to cry when he saw you, but Carol didn't cry until Mary came for her. When Danny got sick and ran outside, Carol told one of the officers to take him a cold washcloth. The guy did it."

"I know it was hard for Danny, so soon after his grandpa's death. Carol and Danny may need counseling, but I'm glad she knew what to do. Jaeger planned to kill us both. He kept hitting me, trying to make me tell him where Carol was hiding. I never leave a loaded gun in the house unless it's on my hip or in my hands, but I was so tired the night before, that I forgot to unload."

"Maybe that was God's plan to save you."

"That could be, but what do Mary and the professor think about me being so careless?"

He shakes his head. "Mary said she'll bring the kids to see you this afternoon. Danny was a big help yesterday morning at the house. He used your dad's nail gun and worked like a man. I don't let him use the saw, but he's good at measuring and nailing."

"After Mary brings the kids to visit, will you and Danny go back and work on our house? I want it ready to move into by the time the doctor says my lip is kissable. Now that I know Jaeger is gone, I'm ready to get on with our lives."

He grins and kisses her hand. "You bet I will. I'll see you after church."

Chapter Two

Weak from non-activity and lack of food, Anna finds it difficult to sit up in bed. The nurse promised to help her with a shower, but the clock has ticked away an hour since she left the room. People come and go along the hallway—patients dragging slippers and pulling IV poles with clacking wheels, doctors walking fast, their heels clicking, and nurses with soft-soled shoes squeaking against the waxed tile. Exhausted, she eases back and closes her eyes.

Bart promised to visit at lunchtime. She cannot even drink through a straw, but more than anything, she wants a cola over ice and a shower.

The door opens, and a nurse rushes in. "Sorry. I've been trying to get back, but everything seemed to happen at once. I brought you a clean gown; I'll hang it beside the shower."

Anna leans her head back, so the nurse can run water through her long hair and wash out residues of dried blood without wetting her face and stitches.

Anna pushes the shampoo away and slumps toward the floor.

The nurse throws a towel over her head. "Hang on a minute. Your hair will drip everywhere."

Anna grabs the cold-water handle, holding tight as she slides down the wall. Cold water sprays, soaking the towel. The nurse bumps the showerhead to one side, wraps an arm around

Anna's collapsing body, and eases her to the floor. Another girl rushes in. They half-drag, half-carry her to the bed. When Bart arrives, Anna, wrapped in white cotton blankets, sits in the recliner waiting for the hospital staff to change her bed.

"What happened? You look pale."

Feebly, she lifts a hand and blinks.

An aide answers his question. "She fainted in the shower."

He offers a notepad and pencil.

Anna does not reach for it.

Bart kneels beside her chair and kisses her hand.

A doctor comes through the door in brown dress slacks, tan shirt, brown striped tie, and a starched white smock coat. "I'm Doctor Newhouse, a staff neurologist. Your surgeon suggested we get a brain scan to make sure the beating you took didn't cause a bleed in your brain."

Anna grabs the notepad and scribbles, "I don't have insurance."

"That doesn't matter. The hospital is obligated to care for your needs. Do I have your permission to run the scan? Blink if your answer is yes."

She writes, "I don't have a headache—my blood sugar is low. Can you get a straw through this tape so that I can drink a cola?"

"Are you diabetic?"

She writes, "Hypoglycemic."

He steps to the door and speaks to a nurse. "Check her blood sugar. Call me when you get the result."

The nurse pricks Anna's finger and tests the blood. Looking at the monitor, she raises her eyebrows and leaves the room without saying a word.

The doctor comes back. "You're right. Your blood sugar is

extremely low. The nurse will add glucose to your IV. It's not the same as an ice-cold soda, but it will make you feel better. I'll check with your doctor and maybe before the day is over you can drink soup through a straw." He grins. "And possibly a soda."

Anna blinks and lifts her hand.

The doctor clasps her fingers. "I'll postpone that brain scan, but tomorrow morning, we may run a glucose tolerance test. I'll check on you later." He leaves the room after a quick handshake with Bart.

Bart kisses her cheek. "I need to go see what Danny's doing. I dropped him off at the house after church and left him working. I'll bring him up tonight."

Anna blinks and writes on the notepad. "Did you leave him alone?"

"He has my phone. He'll be fine."

"He's too young to leave alone. What if those bears come out of the woods, looking for more trash to scatter? Child services will nail you to the wall if they find out."

He blows her a kiss and leaves.

Before visiting hours, people from the church start arriving. No one brings flowers, but a few bring checks to help toward her hospital bill. Carol and Mary do not stay long. Mary tells her they will come back after the evening church service.

Sunday night more visitors arrive.

Carol is unusually quiet, but Danny tells Anna about the new porches he and Bart are going to build, and the new carpet a builder from the church donated and helped install that afternoon. "All the rooms are different colors, but they're pretty. The living room and your bedroom are brownish. My carpet is navy blue, and Carol's is red."

Quickly, she writes, "Three bedrooms? When did that happen?"

Bart's face reddens. "Yesterday morning. We need to paint the walls. I wanted to surprise you. Danny and I put a dividing wall on the west end and separated that into two rooms—each one big enough for a bed and nightstand."

Anna stares with her unbandaged eye and does not lift the pencil.

"We didn't need such a big bedroom, and it didn't cost much to add two small guest rooms. Mr. McGee, from church, gave us plywood and molding. Some others gave us scrap lumber, paint, and caulking. I stored some in the old garage until we can use it. The kids want to help build bunk beds next week. We'll have room for friends to visit."

"Carol and I love our rooms and the soft carpet," Danny says. "That builder may have enough leftover vinyl to cover the kitchen and bathroom. If he does, he'll bring it this week."

"Danny, you and Carol have to understand that Mary and Professor Dugan are not going to let you live at the cabin. You'll only get to visit on weekends."

"We know. They're not our rooms all the time—only when we visit."

Anna writes answers to questions until her hand aches. When everyone leaves, the nurse apologizes as she puts restraints on Anna's hands to keep her from accidentally pulling at the bandages during the night.

* * * * *

Monday morning, Anna feels better. After a nurse removes

the restraints, Anna writes on a pad, "I want to try taking a shower if you'll stand by to catch me."

"I'll get you a fresh gown and call the girls to change your bed. Lie there until I come back."

This time, she gets a good shower and does not slide down the wall. She is sitting in a chair reading the Bible when the doctor comes in and looks at her chart.

"You have a healthy color to your face, and the nurse tells me you didn't faint this morning. I've ordered a high protein liquid diet that you can drink through a straw until we get the tape off your mouth. I told them to flavor and season it well, and you can have fruit smoothies twice a day. It's not the tastiest diet, but maintaining your beautiful face is worth it." He pats her shoulder. "I'll cancel the order for a brain scan unless you start having headaches. I believe you were right about your low blood sugar."

Anna sits thinking, wanting to smile. A doctor admitted that she was right.

Finally, the nurse removes the bulky bandage from her eye, replaces it with a smaller one, and removes most of the tape from her mouth, but adds a bandage before visiting hours. The doctor tells her, "I don't want you laughing, kissing or opening your mouth wider than a quarter of an inch. We can't take a chance on opening those cuts."

Mary and Carol arrive in the evening. Carol snuggles close and whispers, "I'm helping build your new house. Today, we worked on the porches. Bart said Danny and I could print our names on one corner of the concrete."

Anna writes, "I wish I could help."

Tuesday, Anna is resting on fresh sheets when Bart, Danny,

and Carol arrive. Bart sits on the edge of her bed and takes her hand. "I've got bad news. Late yesterday, Danny and I found a marijuana patch on one end of the property. It's near the creek, and someone's taking good care of it."

She beats on the bed until he hands her the notepad.

"What are you going to do? Do they know you found the patch?"

"We didn't see anyone, and we left as soon as we realized what the plants were. Detective Miller is supposed to meet us here to talk about it."

Two swift knocks push the door open a crack. Bart calls, "Come in."

Detective Miller waves and, with a grin, shakes his head "Anna, why can't we keep you out of trouble?"

She extends her hand. He gives it a gentle squeeze.

"I alerted the Narcotics division. "Investigators are there now. I talked to them before coming inside. They found two boys, one about five or six, the other around fourteen. They carried watering cans, a hoe, and a shovel. The boys came to water, but the plants were gone. There were no traces of the plants, except holes in the ground. The largest boy said a man told them he would give them two dollars a day to keep the plants watered. He owes them for thirty-two days."

Bart shakes his head. "There's not a chance of them returning to pay the kids."

"I'm sure of that. They probably had a surveillance camera and decided to harvest the crop after it detected you and Danny. I don't think they'll come back. Next summer, they'll find another fertile spot in a remote area near a creek."

"I hope they've left for good. I thought Anna and I were

building our house in a safe place where Carol and Danny could play without worry."

Danny grins. "Yeah, up to now, we only watched for bear, mountain lions, and rattlesnakes."

Bart gives him a friendly tap on the head. "Detective Miller, did those kids know what they were watering?"

"The largest one said the men told them it was okra, but he knew it wasn't the same kind of plant as his grandma's okra. They wanted to earn a few dollars and didn't care what the men were growing. The detectives said the boys were ragged, and the youngest looked as if he had been crying. I guess it was quite a letdown to find the plants gone and know they wouldn't get paid for their work."

"Will you ask the Narcotics men to check all along the creek between the two main roads? I don't want Carol and Danny riding horses near a marijuana patch."

"I'll ask, but I don't know what's on their schedule. They will probably fly a helicopter over that area and look from the air. Those guys will not want to walk those hills in this heat and subject themselves to rattlesnakes, ticks, and chiggers."

"I can't blame them." Bart lifts his jean leg and scratches his ankle. "Danny and I got into a patch of chiggers."

"How is your house progressing?"

"Good. Yesterday, Danny and I borrowed a cement mixer and poured a couple of small porches. We can move in when Anna gets well. We'll send you a wedding invitation. It won't be a fancy event, but the churchwomen said they'll prepare a potluck meal and a big wedding cake."

"Sounds like the way to go. My sister got married three years ago, and it cost my parents a small fortune. A wedding should be a celebration of love, not an event to bankrupt parents."

"Neither of us have wealthy parents to foot the bill. Our wedding must be simple."

"Anna, I hope the next time I see you is at your wedding. Take care." He waves and leaves the room.

Bart sits on the edge of the bed. Danny and Carol slide into chairs on each side. Anna writes on her notepad. "Danny, has Bart asked you to stand beside him as best man?"

Danny nods. "He did, but I don't have a suit that fits."

"Don't worry; it's not a formal wedding. Mary will see that you have proper clothes."

"Okay, I'll do it."

"Carol, I want you for my maid of honor."

She nods and smiles. "I'll ask Mama to get me a new dress."

"Now, we have to set a date, and I can't do that until my lip gets well, but it's healing. The doctor said I can go to the Dugans tomorrow."

"Can you come to the cabin and watch me and Danny work?"

"I asked him that—he said, 'No.' He wants me to rest, in an air-conditioned room until my lips heal, but will you drive me by there for a few minutes. I'm eager to see what you've done."

"Send me a text message when the doctor signs the release, and we'll come to get you."

"I wish I knew more about the kids watering those plants. I've never seen strangers on our property."

"There's an old house south of the creek. Danny and I drove by it one day. It needs maintenance, but you can tell someone lives there."

"When I get well, I'll bake a pie for them, and we'll go visit."

Danny touches her arm. "Don't set a pie in the window to cool. Those bears are still around close. We found new tracks in the yard this morning."

"Bears!" She underlines the word. "How many do you think are hanging around?"

Bart paces in front of the window. "My guess is an old sow and two half-grown cubs that came out of the mountains east of Fayetteville. They're hungry this time of year. Blackberries and wild plums are gone, and muscadines are not ripe. Unless they raid trash cans, gardens or an apple orchard, I don't know what they can eat. Danny and I decided not to plant fruit trees; we don't want to tease the bears."

Danny stands at the foot of the bed. "It's a good thing the horses can stay inside that high rock fence at the Dugan house. The man at the feed store said people on the east side of town are having trouble with bears eating their horse and cow feed, especially the sweet feed."

Carol grabs Bart's arm. "Get a hunting license and shoot them. If you get all three, we can put bearskin rugs in all your bedrooms."

"I'll do that. Danny, have you ever been hunting? We might get a deer and make some jerky."

Carol folds her arms across her chest. "I want you to shoot bears. I'm not afraid of deer."

"I'll have to find out when deer and bear season starts in this area. Anna, will you let me and Danny use your guns?"

She takes the pencil and writes fast. "Danny will need to take a hunter's safety class, and you'll have to take turns with the guns when I get well. I renew my hunting license every year. I never killed a deer, but I shot a tom turkey. We ate it for Thanksgiving the year I turned fifteen."

"I remember that. Your mom invited Aunt Alice and me."

Anna puts her hand over her mouth to keep from laughing and stretching the stitches. "I mashed the potatoes and forgot to add salt, but you said you liked them that way. After you went home, Dad said, 'That boy's a true gentleman—no one prefers unsalted mashed potatoes.'"

Chapter Three

Fully dressed, Anna sits reading the Bible for two hours before her doctor arrives.

As always, the color of his clothes match perfectly, his slacks have knife blade creases, and there is not a wrinkle in his starched white smock coat. "Hello, Anna. I think we need to keep you a few more days—to decorate this drab hospital."

She exhales and her shoulders slump before she realizes he is teasing. She grabs the pen and paper. "You caught me off guard. You have to turn me loose. I have a wedding to plan."

He grins. "Okay, let me get some of that tape off, so I can see both of those brown eyes and a little smile before you go. You still have to be careful, no laughing or kissing, and do not put makeup on your face. I want to see you in my office in a week. The nurse will schedule appointments for the next three weeks. Don't skip them. I need to check on your progress."

Bart, Danny, and Carol walk in as Anna taps a text message. "We couldn't wait any longer. Has the doctor released you?"

Bart leans close looking at her face. "The doctor was right; you are as beautiful as ever."

Doing her best not to laugh, she barely smiles. "I'm afraid to talk." Holding her mouth as motionless as possible, she says, "Please, please be serious for three more weeks, and then I can laugh. I have to put a bandage on my mouth and eye every night for a week, maybe two. It looks healed on the outside, but the doctor said it needs more time to heal inside."

Bart bends and kisses the top of her head. "We'll do our best to keep you from laughing."

Bart and Danny carry her things, Carol trots close to the wheelchair as the nurse pushes Anna out to the car. "I can hardly wait to see our little house."

Bart constantly talks until they stop in the driveway. "There it is."

Danny jumps out and runs around to open Anna's door. "I want you to see the front porch first."

"Oh, I love it, and the rocking chair—I can rock as I read to you and Carol."

Bart holds one of Anna's hands; Carol holds the other. "Mama helped me choose curtains for your kitchen. I bought them with my money."

"They are beautiful. I love blue and yellow. My mama's dishes are blue. Oh, the tablecloth matches. You've all done such a wonderful job. Thank you."

Bart bends to remove Anna's shoes. "I want you to walk on our new carpet and feel the softness."

"It's wonderful, like walking on air."

"It was supposed to go in a congressman's bedroom, but his wife changed her mind about the color and paid to get another after she'd ordered this, so we got it for almost nothing. Danny and Carol's carpets are remnants from another house. We got them free, but they're soft."

Carol puts an arm around Anna's waist. "Look at Danny's curtains. They have birds and waterfalls—mine have red poppies. Mama bought our curtains."

"I love them."

Bart leads her toward the kitchen door. "You have to see the back porch, but after that you need to sit and rest."

"Oh, a porch swing. We can sit here and have morning coffee. It's perfect."

"Don't smile!" The kids chime. "We'll do all the smiles for three weeks. Go sit on the front porch; we'll bring your lunch."

Sitting in the rocker, she leans her head back to relax. A gunshot echoes from farther down the creek. "It's not hunting season. Why would someone be shooting?" A second shot echoes across the hills, sending a chill along Anna's spine.

Bart grins. "Maybe they shot a big snake."

Danny's eyes widen. "Or a bear."

Carol comes outside with a tray of sandwiches. "I hope someone killed that big bear."

Danny stands, looking across the valley. "I don't! I want the bear skin for my room."

Bart brings four bottles of orange soda and a bag of corn chips. "Lunch is served. Eat fast, kids; we have work to do this afternoon."

After Bart says grace, they see two boys running toward them. The oldest holds a rifle. Gasping for air, they stop at the edge of the yard. "Sir, we shot that old mama bear, and she fell in the cemetery, right on top of our grandpa's grave. Will you bring your truck and drag the carcass to our yard and help me hang it, to skin?"

"Have you ever skinned a bear?" Bart asks.

"I helped Grandpa skin deer, and I helped with butcherin' hogs."

"That's good. You'll have to show me what to do. I've never skinned anything."

"We need to hurry, or she'll spoil in this heat. If we can get her skinned and cut into chunks, we can put the meat in refrigerators to chill until we can slice and store it in Grandma's deep freeze. We have two refrigerators, both almost empty 'cept for bottles and jars."

"What about the game warden? It's not bear season."

"That bear was chasin' my brother. I had to shoot it. You can see where she broke our apple tree and wrecked the tomato patch. If the game warden comes around, I'll tell him you didn't have anything to do with killin' it."

Bart turns to Anna. "I've got to help them. Will you be okay here with Carol? If you get tired, take a nap on the new carpet. A couple of sleeping bags and some pillows are in the bedroom."

"We're fine. Do you have a gun, in case another bear comes by?"

"In our bedroom closet." He looks around frantically. "Let me grab my hunting knife, and a hand saw for the bones."

Bart and Danny chug their soda, drop the empty bottles near a tree and run looking for supplies, chewing the last big bites of their sandwiches. Bart turns to Carol with a grin. "Maybe that sandwich will hold me until I can eat some of that pie you promised to make."

The oldest boy follows Bart. "Sir, do you have a chain? Grandpa's ropes are old. It'll take a chain to hold that big carcass, and some clean white trash bags will be handy for storing the meat."

"I have a couple of short chains that should work. Carol, while I get the chains, grab a box of white trash bags from under the sink. Get him that new box of zipper bags from the cabinet, and the first aid kit—who knows when a sharp skinning knife might slip." Bart runs for the chains leaving the kids searching for bags.

They toss supplies into the truck. "I think that's all we'll need. I'll be glad to share the meat with you, but I don't want it to ruin. Bear meat is good. This one should keep us fed all winter."

Anna calls to the boys. "Take these sandwiches to eat on your way. You'll be starved before you get that bear cut up."

The youngest one runs over and grabs them. Taking a bite from inside the sandwich wrap and mumbling thanks as he turns to go.

"Take the soda. You'll need something to wash that down."

He takes two sodas and runs to the truck.

Bart starts the motor. "Take care," he yells, "We'll be back as soon as possible."

Anna sighs as the truck roars along the road. "Carol, do you have any more sandwich meat and bread? I gave away your lunch."

"That's okay. He looked hungry. There's bread, and cheese in the fridge. No more soda, but Bart bought some chocolate vitamin drinks for you."

"A vitamin drink is all I want. Can you eat a cheese sandwich with chips?"

She nods. "I like cheese and chips."

"I wish I were well, so we could help, but they have a big job that will last all afternoon."

Carol wrinkles her nose. "I'm not sorry I missed it. I bet that old bear stinks something awful."

"I don't doubt that. It's nice here on the porch, in Grandma

Tucker's rocker. It was sweet of Danny to let me use it."

"Danny said he wished you were his real mama. He doesn't remember her and doesn't know what happened to her or his dad. He said Jim kept promising to tell him but never did."

"He's a good boy. We're lucky to have him as our friend."

"After you, he's my best friend."

"He's getting almost as good as you at dancing. I think you are both natural born dancers."

Carol giggles. "It's fun. Danny and I like the fast dances best."

"So do I." Anna leans back and fans her face with a sale paper that Carol removed from the new mailbox.

"Do you want to go inside and rest? I'll spread the sleeping bags and pillows for you."

"Thanks, but I think it's cooler on the porch. I feel a breeze. Do you want to read me a story? I noticed storybooks in your room."

"I would rather you give me a cooking lesson. I made a list and asked Bart to buy groceries. He said he was afraid the bears would break in and eat them, but he got them. If you'll sit in your chair and tell me what to do, I can make a peach cobbler."

Anna blinks. "What did you ask him to buy?"

Carol stands straight with hands on her hips. "I've been watching you cook. I know what goes in peach pie. I told him to get flour, sugar, cinnamon, sliced canned peaches, butter, and margarine."

"Anna turns her head to look at Carol. "Did Bart buy canned biscuits, the flaky kind?"

She nods. "I told him that's the kind you use on cobbler pie."

"After the pie, I can make us a Mexican dinner if you'll tell me what to do. I've watched you make quesadillas, so I asked him to get canned white chicken, cheese, onions, green peppers, and flour tortillas. I didn't ask for beans and rice, but he got rice that you boil in the bag, and some canned refried beans."

"That sounds good; with tiny bites, I can eat that. I'm still weak from my hospital stay, so you'll have to do it all, and you'll get tired before it's finished."

"I know, but I want to do it. Can I make the pie first? We can rest before we put it in the oven."

"Okay. Did Bart bring my dishes, and pots and pans up here?"

"He didn't bring your mother's china. Mama told him to save that until you have a bigger house with room for your china cabinet."

"Okay, see if you can find a white bowl with little blue flowers on the outside."

Carol runs to the cabinet and yells. "I found it."

Anna sits at the table. "Open the can of peaches and pour it in the bowl."

"How do I open the can?"

Anna shows her how to use the new electric can opener. She mixes peaches, cinnamon, sugar, and a tablespoon of flour inside the bowl. "Get a stick of margarine and a can of biscuits from the refrigerator and bring me a knife and a cutting board."

Anna slices the margarine into thin slices. "Carol, place this margarine over the peaches. Now, open the biscuits, pull apart the layers and place them over the margarine, and put more margarine slices over the biscuit dough."

"Good job. Now get a cup and mix a teaspoon of cinnamon into a one-third cup of sugar and sprinkle it over the top of the buttered biscuit dough."

"Show me the one-third mark on the cup." Carol does as Anna tells her.

"Put it in the cold oven, turn the oven on and set the knob pointing at 350."

Carol frowns at Anna. "You always get the oven hot before you put the pie inside."

Anna gives her an OK sign. "You remember well. I don't want you trying to lift a heavy bowl of pie into a hot oven. Don't worry, your pie will taste good. I bet Bart and Danny won't stop until every bite is gone."

Carol smiles and throws Anna a kiss. "Do you think other kindergarten kids know how to make a peach cobbler?"

"I bet there is not another one in this state."

"Can we make the quesadillas now?"

"Get a plastic bowl and put two sticks of margarine in it, put plastic wrap over the top, and set it outside on that big rock."

"In the hot sun?"

"Yes, so it will melt. I don't want you lifting hot margarine from the stove. You can make quesadillas when it melts. Today, you can bake them."

"Bart bought lemonade mix. Do you want me to make you some?"

"That sounds good. Make a pitcher full, and we'll have the rest for supper."

Carol does not need direction to mix the lemonade. She has made that before.

"Let's lock the doors and take a nap while your pie cools. It is a beautiful pie and smells delicious."

Carol spreads the sleeping bags in her bedroom where a cool breeze billows the curtains. "I hope we don't nap too long and not have the food ready when Bart and Danny get back."

"I don't think we will, but I need to rest for a while."

Anna wakes to Carol shaking her. "Wake up. I think those bears are in the yard. I hear something growling."

Rushing to get a gun from the closet, Anna shouts, "Carol, get a pan and beat on the bottom with a big spoon." From the kitchen window, she has the gun aimed at one of the bears when Carol hits the pan. The fuzzy critter jumps and runs for the woods. The second cub lifts its margarine-smeared nose from the bowl and follows; his cries echo against the mountain.

Anna unloads the gun. "Well, so much for our sun melted margarine. Do we have more sticks?"

"One, but we have a tub of soft butter."

Anna returns the gun to the closet. "We can use that. I guess we should get started since we don't know how long it will be before those guys get back."

"Are we going to put the butter in the sun?"

"Not this time. Wash your hands with soap while I melt it on the stove in a skillet. See if you can find a couple of cookie sheets and a roll of aluminum foil to spread over the cookie sheets." Within an hour, they have quesadillas, rice and refried beans ready for supper.

"I wish they were here now. I'm getting hungry, but I bet they're sick of smelling that stinky old bear, and seeing all that blood."

"I don't doubt it."

"Do you mind if I call Mama on your phone? She might get upset if she comes home, and we're not there."

"That's a good idea. We should have called her earlier."

"It's okay; she knows your number. She would have called

you if she were worried."

"Mama, I'm at Anna's house. Bart and Danny went to help some boys that shot a bear. It was chasing the youngest boy, and his big brother shot it."

She looks at Anna and smiles. "No, they're all right. Bart will help them cut it up, so they can eat it. Anna said not to tell anyone because the boys might get into trouble—it's not the season to shoot bears."

She stands nodding her head. "First let me tell you something. I made a peach cobbler all by myself, and I made chicken and cheese quesadillas and refried beans for supper. No, I didn't touch anything hot. No, I didn't fry them; I'll turn the oven on to melt the cheese when it's almost time to eat. We tried to melt the butter in the sun, but bears came along and ate it. I ran them away when I beat on a pan with a spoon. Here she is. I love you too. Bye."

She hands the phone to Anna. "Hello, Mary. Don't worry about Carol. I'm teaching her to cook, but I didn't let her lift anything hot. I think she could have done it without my help. She watches me cook and makes mental notes." Anna smiles and touches her cheek to keep from laughing.

"They were cubs. A neighbor boy shot the sow bear because it was chasing his brother. Yes, the doctor told me to go home and rest, but I'm fine. Carol and I locked the doors and took a nap on the sleeping bags. It was cool enough with a breeze blowing in the window. If you and the professor want to go out for dinner, don't worry about us. Carol, Danny, and I will eat here with Bart. We would have made enough for you, but Bart only had one can of chicken in the pantry. We'll be home later. Oh, thanks for the pretty curtains. They are perfect. Bye."

The sun is setting before Bart returns with all three of the boys. Carol puts a wash pan and a bar of antibacterial soap on a stump beside the well house. "Here are hand towels, one for each of you. Anna said to scrub your face and arms and sit on the porch. We don't have enough chairs inside, but we'll fix your plates and bring them to the porch."

Chapter Four

The youngest boy merely nods when Bart introduces them and says nothing during the meal, except "Thank you." The older boy speaks for them both.

Carol asks, "What grades are you going to be in when school starts?"

"We ain't goin' this year. Our granny is awful sick; we can't go off and leave her alone all day. We need to go so that I can check on her."

Anna reaches to touch his arm. "You have to go to school. If you don't, Social Services will come looking for you. Your grandma and you boys will all be in trouble."

He pulls away. "How'll they know? Are you gonna turn us in?"

"No, not me. Where did you go to school last year?"

"Fayetteville."

"Hank, they have a record of you, and will send an investigator if you don't show up this year."

"We can't go. We don't have school clothes, and Granny's too sick to go shoppin'. I ain't about to go lookin' like this and have kids makin' fun."

"If your granny's too sick to go shopping, how do you get groceries?"

"I take a list to the store on the highway, and the grocer charges it to Granny's credit card. She pays our electric bill and everything with her Visa. She has money from Grandpa's retirement, but she's not able to go shoppin'."

"She can order clothes for you online. Do you have a computer?"

"Grandpa's—I know how to use it."

"Ask your grandma how much you can spend. And then go online to any of the major stores, type in what you want, the sizes, colors, etc. and get her to pay with her credit card. If you need help, come by and I'll show you what to do on my laptop."

"I may do that. I don't want to get Granny in trouble, and Bill needs a few years of school. He can count, but he can't read anything except his name. He's supposed to start kindergarten. Schoolin' wouldn't hurt me either if we can get some decent clothes."

The youngest boy stands. "Hank, are you about ready to start home? It'll be black dark 'fore we get there."

"Yeah, we better git. Those cubs might come after us in the dark. Thanks for the food. That pie was special. I want you to tell me how to make it sometime. Since Grandma got sick, I do the cooking, and I ain't never made a pie."

Bart stands. "I'll drive you home. You don't need to walk around in these hills after dark. Carol, you and Danny clean the dishes. We need to get Anna home. She looks awful tired."

Bart stops at the Dugans' front door and holds onto Anna until she is sitting on the couch. "Sit here; I'll take your bag to your room. Mary, do you have some soup that Anna can drink through a straw? She only ate a few refried beans for supper. I should have bought soup for the cabin, but I didn't mean to keep her there all day."

"Sure, I'll heat it. Carol, the dinner you made sounds

delicious. You'll have to make that for us one evening, but right now, you need to take your bath." Mary leaves for the kitchen; Carol trudges toward the stairs.

Bart taps Danny on the shoulder. "You need to head for the shower. We had a long day, and another tomorrow. I'll drive you around to the garage. You can get ready for bed while I come back and talk with Anna about the house and wedding plans."

Anna reaches to hug Bart as he comes near her chair. "Do you want a cup of soup?"

"No, a shower and a soft bed, but I want to visit with you for a while. It seems like weeks since we've had time alone. I'll be back in a few minutes."

Anna sips her soup while waiting. Tomato with beef broth never tasted so good.

Quietly, Bart slips inside. "I'm sorry about leaving you at our house, but I knew those boys needed help. They have a freezer full of bear steak. I helped cut and package the meat after it cooled in the fridge. They tried to give me part of it, but at that moment, I was ready to become a vegetarian."

"I can imagine. How did Danny handle it?"

"Good. I think it bothered me the most. Danny said that once he helped his grandpa skin a deer, and he had helped clean chickens. They laughed when I told them the only thing I'd skinned was an onion."

She sets her cup on the table. "What did they do with the bear skin?"

"They didn't want it. Danny wants it, but he doesn't know how to make it into a rug. A guy that was in my history class last year is studying taxidermy. I called him about the skin, and he said he'll tan it for free if I buy the supplies. He wants to use it for a class project. Don't tell Danny. I want to surprise him. The supplies won't cost nearly as much as having it done at a taxidermy shop."

"Where is it now?"

He looks at the floor and, with a red face, turns toward her. "It's in a black trash bag. Before we left the cabin, I put it in the refrigerator. Tomorrow, I'll take it to my friend."

She blinks and makes an OK sign. "As long as I don't have to touch it."

"I figure it'll be a few days before you and Carol come back. You need to rest and follow the doctor's instructions."

"I was surprised that Bill and Hank came back with you."

He laughs. "I guess they came for supper or the pie they heard me mention to Carol. They just climbed in the truck when we got ready to go. I didn't see or hear any noise from the house. If their granny was there, she didn't come out of the bedroom all day. Hank told us we couldn't use the bathroom because the toilet was broken. He said Granny has a potty chair beside her bed, but he and Bill go to the barn. I was glad Carol stayed with you."

"She was excited about cooking. I appreciate my mama even more now that I'm teaching Carol. It's much easier to do than it is to tell someone."

"Hank wants you to teach him. He said he was tired of eating beans and tuna out of cans."

She runs her fingers across her forehead and down the side of her face. "He worries me. Bill seems like Danny was at first—a frightened little boy. Hank reminds me of Jim. I don't think he trusts anyone, and his tough act tells me he's experienced a lot of sadness."

"Let's try to get them to go to church with us."

"That's a good idea." She giggles, slaps her hand on her cheek, and mumbles, "If we keep attracting stragglers, pretty soon we'll have our own boy's camp."

Bart's eyebrows go up, and he shakes his head. "I don't know if we can afford groceries to feed them all. Those boys can put away the food, but I'd hate to tell them they can't eat with us."

A faint smile curves her lips. "We may have to start buying dried beans and rice in fifty-pound sacks, and season it with some of their bear meat."

He grins. "We'll manage. Anna, you are the most unselfish girl I've ever met. Everyone loves you, but none more than me."

"I love you too, but you better go check on Danny and get some rest. Come by for lunch tomorrow. Carol will make sandwiches and lemonade."

He hugs her tight and kisses her cheek. "I'll probably take sandwiches, and come by later in the afternoon."

"You better make enough for Hank and Bill. I have a feeling they've adopted you."

"I can feed them if they'll work. From that scrap lumber, Danny's going to help build a storage shed for the lawnmower and yard tools. Have you noticed him calling it our house?"

She nods. "I noticed. We may have an instant family whether we can afford it or not."

"And we're not married yet."

She smiles a thin smile and puts her hands on her cheeks to prevent it from spreading. "You and Danny be careful and watch for bears. Those cubs are big, and could be dangerous."

"I'll have a gun nearby, but those bears don't worry me as much as Hank and Bill. There's something unusual about that situation. Hank told Danny and me not to go in the house because of his sick Grandma. I asked Hank how long she had been sick and if we should take her to the doctor. He got agitated and said, 'She's grieving over grandpa. We don't want anyone in the house to bother her."'

"That's reasonable, but she may be drowning her grief in a whiskey bottle."

"I did notice several wine bottles in the trash can."

"Well, let it go. We'll try to help them as much as we can."

With a hug and a light kiss on her cheek, Bart goes out the door.

The next morning, Mary is in the kitchen early, cooking breakfast and giving Carol instructions in helping Anna. "Don't ask Anna to teach you to cook. She needs to rest and get well. You can learn to cook after she heals."

Carol frowns and puts her arm around Anna. "This week, I'll take care of her."

"Anna, if you need anything, ask Carol to call my office. I'll come home if necessary."

"We're fine. I'm a lot stronger than when I left the hospital."

Mary glances at her watch. "I have to rush. There's plenty of fruit in the bowl, ham and cheese in the fridge, and different flavors of soup that you can warm in the microwave. Take care, I love you both." After a hug for each girl, she leaves for work.

The door pops open. "I forgot to tell you, that I ordered clothes online for Danny and Carol. UPS should deliver them today or tomorrow. It's fine for them to try them on, but don't remove any tags until I see how they fit. If you can get Hank and Bill's sizes, I'll order clothes for them to wear at the wedding. They're your neighbors and friends, so we have to invite them." The door closes, and she leaves without waiting for an answer.

"Carol, did Mary take that bag of old clothes and donate it to the Church Closet? It contained some of Danny's old clothes and shoes. Bill may be able to wear them; he's tall for his age and Danny's short."

Carol jumps up and runs to open the door going into the garage. The light is still on after Mary closed the automatic door. "Nope, it's sitting in the corner. Do you want me to drag it inside, so we can look?"

Anna nods and Carol drags a big black garbage bag through the door. "I'll spread them on the floor. Tell me which ones to save." Within minutes, they have a sack of clothes that they think Bill can wear. "Some are small. Danny must have saved them for a year or more."

The morning goes quickly. Carol uses the blender to make banana smoothies for Anna and herself. She feeds and waters her dog, Curly, and the horses, Polka and Apple. Anna sits in a chair watching Carol take turns riding the mares. Apple, younger than Polka, is gentle, lean, and fast. She has a lot of potential for barrel racing.

Coming inside for a drink, Carol sits to cool, before going back outside.

"Sister-friend, I need to find a dress. I wore Mama's dress at the wedding with Jaeger—his mother must have found it in Mama's chest-of-drawers. I remember seeing grandma's wedding dress in an old trunk. We moved that trunk to the basement; I hope her dress is still inside and that it will fit me. I'm thinner after not eating solid food for so long."

"You'll probably have time to shop for a dress."

"Carol, turn the horses loose and come with me. I want to look in Bart's basement apartment for my Grandma's trunk and see if her wedding dress is in there."

Carol catches up to Anna before she gets to the garage. "Will Bart not care for you going into his apartment?"

"He shouldn't. We'll be married in a couple of weeks. Besides, I'll not bother his things. I want to look in my grandma's trunk. Mama always kept it locked. I may have to get a locksmith to make a key. I'm hoping that Jaeger's sister didn't find a way to get into it. I only remember seeing it open one time. I was a little girl when mama showed me a beige colored lace dress wrapped in blue paper. She told me it was Granny's wedding dress."

"In the garage, Daddy has an old trunk with his dad's things inside. I watched him open it with a hairpin. Maybe you can do that."

"Do you have a hairpin?"

She nods. "In my playhouse. I use them in my dolls hair. I'll go get a couple."

The lock pops open when Anna twists the pin inside. She sits staring at the open trunk, eager, yet apprehensive of disturbing the contents. Gently, she takes a bundle wrapped in blue paper and asks Carol to put it on Bart's bed. Next is a bundle of letters with Grandpa's name over the address of a military base. Carol places them on the bed. A large brown envelope with a note on the outside in her mother's handwriting is under an old Army coat.

Tears roll down Anna's cheeks as she holds the note.

Carol stares at her. "I don't know what you read, but you have to stop crying. Tears might ruin the stitches on your eye."

She stomps her foot. "I mean it. Stop crying. Come outside. I'm getting hungry; we have to make lunch."

> Anna,
>
> If you find this note, it is because I am not around to give you the contents of this package. Your grandma worked and bought war bonds while your grandpa was away in the war. They gave them to me as a wedding present, with directions to cash and use as needs arose. When they fully matured, your dad and I cashed them and bought stocks that have grown in value over the years. Darling, use them for school, or as needs in your life arise.
>
> Love,
> Mama and Daddy

Anna looks at Carol and wants to laugh. "All right. I'm hungry too. Bart and Danny might come to eat with us if Hank and Bill are not there."

"I bet they're not coming. He's probably fixing lunch for those boys. I'll make you some soup and another smoothie, and I'll have a sandwich and a smoothie."

Anna replaces the trunk's contents, except for her grandma's lace dress, and snaps the lock. "I want to try this dress on and see if I can wear it."

"Do you want me to carry it for you?"

Anna clutches the blue paper wrapping to her chest. "Thanks, but I want to hold it."

"I'll come down to help with lunch in a few minutes. I can't wait to see if this dress fits." Anna takes her grandmother's wedding dress to her room and places it on the bed.

She tosses her shirt on a chair and steps from her jeans. The zipper slides open without a catch after being in the trunk for years. Anna slips into the beige sheath.

Carol bounds up the stairs and stops in the doorway. "Do you want me to zip it?"

"Please do." Anna kneels on one knee so that Carol can zip all the way to the neck.

"Carol, I love you very much; thank you for saving my life."

Carol frowns. "Jaeger wanted to kill both of us. I held the gun, but I don't remember pulling the trigger. I tried to hold it still like Bart said when he was teaching Danny, but it kept shaking. I thought I heard someone say, 'Hold it still.' Then the gun went off." Her chin comes up, and she has a defiant look. "I think your angel pulled the trigger."

"Maybe it was your angel."

She shrugs. "I wanted to pull it." She looks at the floor and hugs herself. "But I don't think I did. One of our angels killed him because he was bad." She pauses. "Mama wants me and Danny to see a counseling doctor at her office, but I don't want to. I'm not sad he's dead. It was him or us."

"It doesn't matter who pulled the trigger. We know God's angels were watching to keep us safe."

Anna kicks off her shoes and stretches across her patchwork quilt. I need to rest a few minutes. Running her hand across the quilt, she remembers her mama sewing dresses and quilting with different fabric pieces. "This one is from a dress Mama made for me to wear in a Christmas play—in fifth grade." She closes her eyes and remembers her mom and dad sitting on the first row of the school auditorium. Bart sat beside them.

Chapter Five

Bart's truck pulls through the wide gate of the fence surrounding the five-acre backyard of the Dugan home. Anna asks, "Carol, did you make sandwiches for Bart and Danny?"

"No, but I will." She grabs bread from the bread box and meat from the refrigerator.

Danny, Carol's foster brother, runs inside. "Get the first aid kit. One of those bears got Bill. It would have chewed his arm off if Hank hadn't shot it."

Carol has a bottle of peroxide, a towel, and the first aid kit on the sunroom table when Bart brings Bill inside. "Hank shot one of those bear cubs, but it latched onto Bill before Hank could kill it. If you girls will doctor his arm, Danny and I can help Hank butcher the bear."

Fear in her eyes, Carol is almost yelling when she says, "Sit him in the sunroom. Bill, slide out of that shirt." She adjusts his arm over a white towel and pours peroxide over the wound. "This will kill germs that were on that bear's teeth."

Bill, pale and trembling, asks, "How do you know that?" He shivers as peroxide bubbles.

"That's what Anna said when I skinned my arm." Staring at his face, she asks, "Why was the bear after you?"

"I hit him with a rock. He was in the garden, eatin' our tomatoes."

"Was the other bear eating them too?"

He shakes his head. "She was after apples, but she ran off when I beat on a pan and yelled. Bigfoot, that's what I've been callin' the biggest one, wouldn't run, so I hit him with a rock. He spun around, came after me and laid his teeth onto my arm as I ducked behind a tree. That's when Hank shot him with Grandpa's rifle. I thought I was a goner. I'm sure glad that Hank's a good shot." He clenches his fist as the cold clear liquid froths. "Grandpa was gonna teach me to shoot—but he died before I could learn." Additional words seem to hang in his throat.

"You better leave those bears alone. Wasn't that old mama bear chasing you when Hank shot her?"

"Yeah, but I didn't throw anything at that old sow. I just happened to be between her and a cub." He grits his teeth and closes his eyes as Carol pours on more medicine.

Anna watches Carol repeatedly pouring the peroxide on his arm.

"As long as this bubbles, it's killing germs," Carol says.

Anna lifts the neighbor boy's shirt and resists holding her nose. The shirt is sweaty, dirty and has blood down the side. "Bill, I want you to go upstairs and soak for a while in the bathtub with antibacterial soap. Then I'll put medicine on that bite. Getting a scratch or a cut clean is very important." She pauses to look at the thin child and wonders if he has the basic skills needed to start kindergarten along with Carol.

"We found some of Danny's clothes that I think will fit you. I'll set them in the bathroom. You can choose anything you want. They are all too small for Danny. Toss your dirty clothes outside the door and I'll put them in the washer. There are socks, underwear, and even some shoes in that sack. Some will be too big—you can save them for later."

Anna fills the tub, adds soap, sets a bottle of kids' shampoo on the edge and drags the bag of clothes inside the room. Before leaving, she tosses some rubber fish into the tub. "You can play as long as you want, just don't splash water all over the room. Wash your hair, and behind your ears. Come downstairs when you finish. You and Carol can have milk and cookies while I put medicine on your arm."

"I won't be long." He closes the door as Anna goes downstairs.

Carol whispers to Anna, "His grandma must be awful sick for Hank not to wake her and tell her about that bear hurting Bill."

Anna nods. "It appears those boys have adopted Bart. Since the first day they came asking him to help with that big sow bear, they run to him as if he were a close relative."

"He's easy to love."

Anna is sitting in the sunroom when Bill comes dragging the bag of clothes down the stairs. He is wearing jeans, a red shirt and a pair of blue sneakers. "These clothes fit. Are you sure Danny won't mind me having them? I could wear these to school."

"Danny wants you to have them. Let me see your arm. It needs antibiotic cream and a sterile bandage." Anna wipes hair away from his forehead. "Danny's going for a haircut tomorrow; do you want to go? It's two-for-one-price day. It won't cost a penny extra."

He nods. "Grandpa always took us for haircuts. I miss him."

"I know." She reaches to hug him. "My parents died last

year; I miss them too."

He wraps his unscratched arm around her, lays his head on her shoulder and hugs. "Grandma used to hug me, but since she . . . ." A ringing phone interrupts. He backs away to sit in a chair as Anna stands to answer the phone.

Carol takes the package of cotton balls and a tube of antibiotic cream from Anna's hand and applies the medicine to Bill's arm.

"That doesn't even burn. The stuff Grandma put on cuts burned awful bad."

Bart calls, "Anna can you find freezer bags and plain white trash bags for chilling the bear meat."

"I'll get the bags, but I don't know about putting bear meat in Mary's freezer. Put all you can in our refrigerator's freezer and the top of your apartment refrigerator. I wish those boys had room for it in their Grandma's deep freeze."

Anna lays the phone in the cradle and slides into a chair. "Carol, I feel weak again. Will you bring me a cola and fix a sandwich for Bill? We need to eat lunch."

Carol runs to the kitchen counter, opens the microwave and removes a cup of soup. "Drink this while I wash my hands, and then I'll get you a cola."

Pausing, Anna looks at Carol.

"Go on, drink it. You can give thanks after I fix my sandwich."

Slowly sipping her soup, Anna marvels at Carol's take charge attitude. "This soup is good."

"I've watched you fix it." Carol smiles and turns to look at Bill. "Is that sandwich okay?"

He pokes the last bite in his mouth, nods and mumbles.

"Good, except I like mustard."

She opens her eyes wide and shrugs. "You watched me make it; why didn't you say so?"

"You didn't ask, and I didn't know you had mustard until I saw it in the fridge after you'd already made the sandwich. Grandma said it's bad manners to ask for somethin' that's not on the table."

"I'll remember for next time, but you should have said something. I would have told you if we didn't have mustard."

He lowers his head. "Thank you, I didn't mean to complain. I bet Hank would like to have a sandwich. We didn't eat breakfast. He needs to go to the store for groceries."

Anna glances at the clock. "It is a few minutes past twelve. Carol, if you and Bill will pack some sandwiches, chips and cookies in the picnic basket, I'll get my purse and car keys. We'll take those guys the freezer bags and some lunch." She turns before going up the stairs. "Put some washcloths and that pack of antibacterial wipes in the basket. They'll need to wash before eating.

Driving along the narrow road, Anna looks sideways at the boy sitting beside her. "Bart said you and Hank are neighbors, but I've never been this far down our road. You'll have to show me where to stop."

"There it is." Bill points. Anna turns into the driveway beside a small house. Dried, white paint curls away from graying boards. Black tar spreads over several places on the roof, bordering unmatched shingles. Faded curtains cover every window.

"Where are they?" Bill asks. "I saw the bear, hangin' from a tree behind the house, but where's Hank and Bart?"

"And Danny?" Carol exclaims from the backseat.

Anna follows Bill around the house. "Maybe your grandma knows where they went."

With a blank look, he pauses to stare at Anna. "Granny, don't know. Hank wouldn't wake her."

Anna scans the yard, panic rising in her chest. "They haven't been gone long. Blood on that skinning knife is still wet."

Bill's face crumples with worry. "Somethin's wrong. Hank wouldn't leave that bear for the meat to ruin, and he wouldn't run off without cleanin' his knife."

Wanting to run and find her fiancé and the two boys, Anna swallows. Her legs quiver and her thoughts are unclear.

Carol, breathing quick and shallow, panic in her childish voice, yells, "Let's go find them."

"Bart will take care of the boys." Her jaw tightens. "It doesn't look so big without the fur." Anna walks near the carcass, still telling herself to stay calm. "Bill, they've skinned it. Do you know what we should do next?"

The boy stands straight, somehow looking older than six. "They must'a been gettin' ready to let it down on that plastic to cut off the hams and shoulders. The rope's tied to that tree." He turns his head sideways and stares. "I guess they thought that old rope was strong enough to hold this small bear." He walks toward the tree.

"Bill," Anna calls. "Wait! Let me check around that tree." She takes the pistol from its holster on her hip and walks slowly, looking at the ground with every step as she crosses the un-mowed yard. Near the tree, a weed sprawls haphazardly, underneath a rattlesnake writhes—severely injured—a bloody rock lies nearby. Taking aim, she shoots the snake's head before releasing the rope to let the bear fall on the plastic.

"Carol, get my phone from the car; call Bart and find out what happened?"

Seconds later, on a nearby tree stump, Bart's phone rings, Anna answers. "Carol, his phone's out here. He probably rushed off and forgot it after that rattler bit one of them. Don't worry; rattlesnake bites are not fatal when treated."

She takes a deep breath and lifts the knife. "Bill, you've watched this before, so tell me what you know. While I work, hold the bags and pray."

Carol runs to them, a sob choking her voice. "Leave that stinking bear. Let's go see if they're okay."

Fighting the panic, Anna ignores the young girl in her care. "I've cut up chickens; I'll just pretend this is a giant chicken."

She glances up, seeing the fear on Carol's face. "Hon, Bart will take care of them. This won't take long and then we'll go. They finished the hard part. Sit on the porch and wait."

When hams, shoulders, and slabs of side meat are inside clean white trash bags, they load it in the car's trunk and drive to the little house that Bart has been trying to complete. Anna removes the refrigerator shelves and turns the temperature to the coldest setting, before slumping into a chair and leaning on the small kitchen table. "Carol, will you and Bill pile those bags inside the fridge?"

Carol runs to get a cold cloth to wash Anna's face while Bill stacks the meat. "I'd help you with almost anything, but I couldn't touch that bloody bear."

"I understand. It was almost too much for me."

Bill has not spoken except to answer questions and give limited advice on cutting the meat. "Anna, will you call the hospital and see if they went there?"

"I don't know the number. Carol, your mom's busy at work, but take my phone, explain this to her, and ask her to call the hospital to see if Bart and the boys are in the emergency room. I'll talk to Mary later. Right now, I feel as if I might faint. Working on that bear used all my energy."

Taking the phone, Carol details the situation to her mama and asks her to find out where the boys are and if they are okay.

Within minutes, Mary calls. Carol stands close, listening to Anna's conversation. "Hank was bitten on the leg by a rattler. Only one fang punctured the fatty part of his calf; the other hit his leather boot. They're treating him at the hospital emergency room. The doctor thinks very little poison entered his leg, maybe none at all, but they want to keep him overnight for observation in case the snake did release venom, or Hank gets an infection. The problem is that Hank will not tell them how to contact his sick grandma, and they need his legal guardian to sign the hospital papers. I'll go over and see if I can help. You need to get home and rest. You're still weak from your hospital stay and don't need to drive in that condition."

"Thank God they're all right." Sentences stream from Anna's mouth. "Did Bart tell you about that cub biting Bill's arm? Carol doctored it with peroxide and antibiotic cream. He didn't want to go to a doctor. It only scratched the surface with its teeth. Bill seems fine now. Hank must have shot it before it bit down." She takes a deep breath before continuing.

"Tell Bart and Hank that I finished the rattler with a bullet and cut up that bear enough to put chunks of meat in our refrigerator. Oh, if the doctor will let Hank have food, tell Bart to get him a sandwich. Bill said they didn't have anything for breakfast. Thanks for your help."

She clicks off the phone and takes another deep breath. "Kids, that rattler bit Hank, but it barely stuck one fang in his leg. The other went into his boot. The doctor said he'll be fine, but they want to keep him overnight."

Bill turns pale again and drops his head onto arms propped on the table.

"Are you okay, Bill?" Anna asks.

"We don't have money to pay for a doctor and hospital."

"Your grandma can take care of the bill when she gets better." Anna walks over to rub his back.

He turns, wraps his arms around Anna, and sobs, "Grandma ain't gonna get better."

"What do you mean? Do you think she's going to die?"

He burrows his face in her shirt sobbing.

"Bill, what's wrong with your grandma?"

He holds tighter and continues to sob. Anna rubs his back and lets him cry for several minutes. At last, Bill pulls away. He sniffs, takes a deep breath and says, "I can't tell you. Hank will get mad."

"Okay, I wouldn't want you to do something to disturb your brother, but if you need to talk to someone, I know how to keep a secret. I'll do everything I can—even help with the doctor bill."

"Would you let me and Hank live with you in your new house?"

"You mean when your grandma can't take care of you anymore?"

He sniffs and turns his face toward the floor. "Yeah, that's what I mean. We can do yard work and raise a garden—we had a good garden 'til those bears got in it. "He sniffs again and rubs the back of a hand over his eyes. "We'll be quiet, so you and Bart can study. Hank's learnin' to cook, but he's not very good yet."

Anna feels a lump clogging her throat and tears stinging her eyes. "Sure, Bart and I will do whatever we can to help. Do you have any aunts or uncles that might have a legal claim and want you to live with them?"

"Only one uncle. He drinks wine and whiskey all the time, and he's mean when he gets drunk. He's Grandma's brother. Grandma made him leave the last time he came to visit 'cause he took money from her purse. I'd never go with him."

Anna sits in a chair next to the thin child and wipes a strand of coal black hair away from his dark eyes. "Bill, I can understand your worry. You and Hank are afraid that the authorities will separate you, maybe send you to different foster homes. Danny was afraid he would have to go to a foster home when his grandpa died, but Mary and Professor Dugan agreed to keep him. The Dugans' are good people. I'm sure they'll help you and Hank when the time comes. They've treated me like a daughter from the first week I came to take care of Carol."

She stands. "We should go back to the Dugan house. I need a nap. I think we all need one. Carol, will you lock the doors?"

At home, Carol goes to her bedroom. Bill climbs on the cot that Anna unfolds for him. With a sigh, Anna stretches out on her bed and closes her eyes—immediately, her mind returns to details of the morning.

Chapter Six

Anna grabs the phone and detects panic in Mary's voice, "Bart's going to get that bear's head for lab tests. The doctors are worried because skunks from our area tested positive for rabies. Little Bill will need treatment if that bear has rabies." Mary pauses.

"There's one more thing. Under pressure from the doctor, Hank confessed that his grandma is dead. She died the night after his grandpa's funeral. The boys were afraid they would have to go to separate orphanages if anyone found out, so they buried her beside her husband. Now the authorities will have to exhume her and perform an autopsy."

Anna trembles. "I suspected something when Bill asked if they could move into the new house with Bart and me."

"Those poor kids. Hank is beside himself with grief, and now worry about what will happen to Bill. He's holding a load of misery inside. I am truly angry with that doctor for getting him upset. I told Hank that we'll take him and Bill. I'm sure Charles will agree."

"It seems unusual for a doctor to be so insensitive to a child's feelings."

"Yes, and I almost had to toss the man from DHS out of Hank's room. He was more than insensitive; he was hateful to that poor boy. I guess they see so many problems that they become hardened to a child's fears."

Bart comes to the back door. "I'm on my way to the hospital with the bear's head. I don't know if they can test it there or if they'll have to send it somewhere." He wipes a hand across his face. "I'm praying it doesn't test positive." He shakes his head and breathes deeply. "I'll drop Danny off here in the late afternoon. I'll need to sleep before going back to relieve Mary. She's scheduled to work tomorrow but insists that one of us spend the night with Hank."

She pats his arm. "I could tell that Hank and Bill were worried about something but thought it was because their grandma was sick."

"Hank needs someone nearby that he can trust. He's carrying a big load for a fourteen-year-old, and that guy from DHS told him he might have to go to a juvenile facility for shooting bears out of season."

"He shot them to protect his brother!"

Bart nods. "Mary came out of her chair when he said that. She told him that he better leave before she reported him for endangering the welfare of a sick child. She was so angry that she called a couple of congressmen, the police chief and someone at the Game and Fish Commission in Little Rock. After that, she called her lawyer and a judge she knows to help her get temporary custody of Hank and Bill."

The following day, Bart brings Hank to the Dugan house before noon. He parks close to the front door and rolls Hank inside in a wheelchair. "Anna, Hank's leg looks bruised and swollen, but the doctor said the bruise was from the tourniquet. He wants Hank to stay off his leg until he checks it again in a few days."

Bart gets a glass of water while she looks at the snakebite.

"Anna, if you should need us, Danny and I'll be working at the house, and Mary said if you have problems, call her, and she'll come home. Professor Dugan signed Hank's release papers, but around two this afternoon someone from the Game and Fish Commission should be here to talk to him."

Seeing worry lines deepen on Hank's face, Anna pats him on the back. "Just tell them why you shot the bears and why you saved the meat—tell them you needed that meat to keep you and Bill from starving."

"I will, and I'll tell them that I'm Cherokee. Grandma had an Indian card, so did Grandpa. Aren't Indians supposed to be able to hunt and fish for food?"

"Maybe on Indian land—I don't know about here. I'll call the Cherokee Office in Tahlequah and see if they can answer some of your questions. Here, kids don't need a license until they are sixteen, but they must take a hunter safety course. I don't know if the same rules apply to Indian boys." She thumbs through a book, looking for a phone number. "Hank, the professor is part Cherokee. I don't know if he has an Indian card, but I heard him tell Mary that his grandmother had one."

Anna punches the numbers and turns on the speaker, so she and Hank can speak to the man at the Cherokee office. "Hello, this is Hank Bird; my dad was Henry J. Bird, a full-blood Cherokee, stationed in Afghanistan with the Army, at the time of his death. Grandma told me one of Dad's friends was a tribal lawyer named Hawk. Can I talk to him? I shot a bear that was after my brother, and I need some help. The Game and Fish people are coming for a meeting about it this afternoon. They may arrest me."

"Do you mean Joe Hawk?"

"I think so. He was in the Army with my dad in Afghanistan."

"Joe Hawk is a busy man, but I'll try to contact him and have him return your call. However, I'll need the names of your parents, grandparents, and their registry numbers. Can you locate their Indian cards?"

"I think so. I've seen Grandma take them from her purse, many times."

"Call me back with the card information as soon as you find it."

He stares at Anna with worry in his eyes.

"Bill can bring her purse to you," Anna says.

He nods. "Sir, I can't walk now because of a snakebite, but my brother can go get them and then I'll call you."

"Good. We'll do our best to help the child of a Cherokee brother. Get that information to me quickly. Maybe Joe can sit with you for the meeting, but postpone it until tomorrow afternoon, if you can. He has a meeting in Fayetteville early in the morning."

Anna calls Bart and asks him to take Bill home to get his Grandma's purse.

When she gets off the phone, she places her hand on Hank's forehead. "You might have a fever. I'll call those people and tell them they'll have to come another day. You need to rest."

His hand goes to his forehead. "I don't feel hot."

She smiles, winks and lifts the phone.

The Game and Fish officer is not pleased with the postponed meeting but finally agrees to meet at two the following day.

"Anna, when my leg gets well, will you help me look for records about my mama? She had a box of my baby pictures and some of her and Dad. I hope Grandma got those."

"Sure, I'll help."

"Thanks. I remember Mama, but Bill can't; he was a baby. I was eight years old when she died. One night she left me with a neighbor, and when I went home the next day, Bill was in bed next to her. He was a tiny wrinkled thing, but I told Mama he was cute. She got sick that day and told me to go get Miss Pearl, the neighbor. Miss Pearl called Grandma to come get Bill and me and asked another woman to stay with us until Grandma got there. Then she took Mama to the hospital."

"Where was your dad?"

"In the army. I remember him comin' home a few times, but he always went back. Mama never came home from the hospital." He pauses to stare out the window. "Grandma said Mama had a bad infection because Bill was born at home, and the midwife couldn't do things like in a hospital. Dad died that same day."

"How did he die?"

"No one told me anything, except that it was an accident. Grandma got upset every time anyone mentioned it. Daddy and Mama were buried in the National Cemetery. After that, Bill and I lived with Grandma and Grandpa. They were good to us, but I missed Mama."

"Danny and Bill have a lot in common. Danny doesn't remember his mama."

Hank's grandpa and grandma's Indian cards are in the purse, along with a card for their son, the boys' father, and birth certificates for Hank and Bill.

While Hank digs through the large purse, Anna puts a cold, gel pack over his injured leg. "We need to call that man at the

Cherokee Center." She pushes numbers, turns on the speaker and hands the phone to Hank.

While waiting to speak, Hank's hand trembles as he holds the phone. "Hello, this is Hank Bird. We found the Indian cards you asked about and one for Henry J. Bird, my dad."

"Was your dad stationed in Afghanistan at the time of his death?"

"Yes, sir. He never got to see my little brother."

"I thought so. Joe Hawk, one of our tribal lawyers, served with your dad in Afghanistan. He volunteered to represent you with your problems. You couldn't hire a better lawyer, but Joe Hawk will not charge you for his services."

The next day Joe Hawk arrives before noon and visits in the sunroom with Hank and Bill while Anna and Carol prepare lunch. Anna listens to the conversation as she works. After a while, she pulls a chair close and sits with them.

The boys are at ease with Mr. Hawk. They talk about hunting, school, and games. Then, without Joe asking, Hank begins to tell about finding Granny. "Mr. Hawk, have you ever found a dead person?"

"I've seen a few. It's not a pleasant thing."

"It was awful. I knew something was bad wrong. When I first saw her, she looked blue." He takes a deep breath and looks away. "She was cold when I touched her. Grandma was so warm the night before while we all cried for Grandpa. Her skin almost felt hot when she hugged me and said everything would be all right. She said she could take care of us with Grandpa's pension. She would order groceries from the store, have them delivered, and pay with her credit card."

A tear rolls down Hank's cheek; he dabs it with his shirt

collar and sniffs. "I didn't know what to do at first. I didn't want to tell Bill about Granny, but I had to. After cryin' for a long time, we sat on the porch and tried to plan. We figured those orphan people would separate us. I couldn't stand to think of that. Mama, Daddy, Grandpa and Grandma are all dead. Bill and I have to stay together." He wraps an arm around his brother.

"Knowin' what those people from the orphanage would do, I put pillows in the bottom of a new aluminum tool chest that Grandpa bought to fit the bed of his compact truck. The tool chest was in the back of the truck, but he hadn't put anything in it, and it wasn't bolted down. As the sun began to set, Bill and I dug beside Grandpa's grave until the ground was level with the bottom of his concrete vault. I wrapped Grandma in a quilt and carried her to the tool chest."

"She must have been heavy for a boy your size."

He shakes his head. "She was tiny, less than what I weigh. I put her on top of the pillows, closed the lid, and I sealed it with caulk so that bugs couldn't get inside. I drove the truck into the cemetery; we slid the chest from the truck and into the grave, covered it with dirt and spread flowers from Grandpa's grave over both of them."

Bill turns to look at Mr. Hawk—his eyes narrow slits with moist lashes. "If Hank goes to jail, I'm goin' too. Wherever he goes, I'm goin'."

Mr. Hawk bows his head and runs a big hand over his face. "I don't think you have to worry about that. It would be a cruel judge to send the two of you to jail."

Bill pulls away from Hank and sits in a chair. "We stayed at the graves the rest of the night. Hank said prayers, and when it got daylight he read from Grandma's Bible."

Mr. Hawk runs his hand through his hair and leans back in his chair. "Tell me about that bear."

Bill straightens his back, his eyes wide. "Hank went to the house to put Grandma's Bible away. The sun was high, and gettin' hot, but I was still sittin' at the grave. Then that big ole' sow bear came waddlin' up, gruntin' like a hog. I took off toward the house. She stopped at the grave and clawed at the dirt. That's when her cubs came from the woods. One ran between the house and me and let out a squeal. The old sow stood and growled loud and deep. I thought sure she was comin' after me, but Hank shot her. She fell right on the graves, kickin' and bellowin'."

Hank interrupts. "I had to shoot her. Bill was too far from the house and between her and a cub. It was a warm day, so we skinned her and put the meat in the refrigerator to cool, and then we cut it up and put it in the freezer. The meat would have ruined if we'd waited for someone from the Game and Fish. Besides, I figured it would keep Bill and me from starvin' this winter."

"What about the cub you shot?"

Hank frowns and adjusts the pillow under his sore leg. "Bill went outside and found one cub bendin' the apple tree and eatin' the last of our apples. The other was in the garden eatin' tomatoes. Bill beat on an old pan with a rock; one ran away, but the one in the tomatoes didn't. Bill threw a rock and hit it in the head, making it mad enough to run after him. It caught up with Bill and raked its teeth down his arm before Bill ducked behind an oak tree, and I pulled the trigger on Grandpa's rifle."

"Did you skin that one and save the meat?"

"We were tryin' when that rattler latched onto my leg. Bart, our neighbor, took me to the hospital. Comin' to bring us some bags, Anna saw the bear, let it down from the tree, and put the meat in Bart's refrigerator. It's not sliced and packaged. The game wardens can have it if they want."

After lunch, Mary and Professor Dugan arrive with their lawyer and two congressmen. They and Mr. Hawk settle into the den before people from Human Services, the Game and Fish Commission, the Prosecuting Attorney's office and the Arkansas Department of Health arrive.

Mr. Hawk stands, takes a small tape recorder from his pocket and places it on an end table. "Hank and Bill, you were not aware that I was recording when you were telling about your Grandma and those bears, but I want to ask your permission to use it as testimony."

The two wide-eyed boys nod. With a distinct southern drawl, Hank says, "It's the truth. You have our permission."

"Okay, you boys can go back to that plate of cookies. I'll call if I need you."

"Gentlemen and Mrs. Dugan, before we begin our discussion, I want you to hear this tape."

Anna hears the soft click of the machine. Everyone is silent until the boys' stories are complete. Speaking in a voice loud enough for Anna to hear clearly, Joe Hawk says, "What judge with a heart would punish these children for trying to survive?"

The man from DHS interrupts. "But laws have been broken."

"Sir, what laws? Hank shot that bear to protect his brother. They saved the meat from spoiling. Otherwise, the County Health Department would have to send a crew to dispose of the rotting carcass, and that might cost more than buying a side of beef. Also, if that bear has rabies, killing it probably saved others a lot of pain."

"But, they should have reported it."

"These are children. They had no transportation and a disconnected phone. Our education system does not provide schooling on Game and Fish Regulations. They simply did what seemed the natural thing to do—preserve the meat." Mr. Hawk clears his throat and stands in the doorway, his large frame filling the opening between the den and hall.

The man from the Health Department speaks, "What about the grandma? Surely they knew that wasn't the proper way to bury her."

"Sir, we are talking about frightened children that knew nothing of embalming and proper funeral procedure. They knew the grave should be deep, so they dug down to the same level as the bottom of Grandpa's vault. They knew the casket should be sturdy and sealed so animals and insects couldn't dig into it—the new toolbox was sturdy, and they sealed it with caulk."

He pauses to look around the room. "Hank knew she was dead when he found her, but he had no idea a licensed physician was supposed to sign a death certificate. We know she had heart problems. This morning, I paid a messenger to deliver a copy of her medical records to this address. They are there." He points. "On top of the bookshelf if you want confirmation of her serious heart condition."

The man from the Health Department says, "It will cost several thousand dollars to exhume her, perform an autopsy, and conduct a proper funeral."

"Why not leave her at peace? Her doctor said he was surprised she lived through her husband's funeral. No fancy casket from a funeral home would be stronger than that toolbox.

You could run over it with a tractor, and it wouldn't cave in, so she doesn't need a vault. Why not prepare a death certificate and let her rest where she is?"

The man from the Health Department shrugs. "That's up to the Prosecuting Attorney."

The representative from the Prosecuting Attorney's office says he has no objection, but he will need to confer with his boss about a final decision.

The Game and Fish Commission officer says, "I'm willing to let the issue drop if we can keep it from the media. We don't want this type of thing to set a precedent."

Everyone nods.

Mr. Hawk stands straighter. "I contend that these kids have suffered far more than any child should. Their dad died in a foreign land in defense of this country. Their mother might not have died if her husband had been home to take her to the hospital. And the combined trauma of losing a son, a daughter-in-law, and caring for two young boys surely added stress to the hearts of two old people."

Everyone stands shaking hands. The congressmen congratulate the other representatives on their wise decisions, thank the Dugans' for their hospitality, and leave.

Mary puts an arm around Hank. "Don't worry, Charles and I will speak for you and Bill. Our home is open to you."

Hank smiles. "Thanks."

Mr. Hawk extends his hand. "A judge will consider what you boys want above the wishes of anyone else. I believe this is your home. Your dad was my friend, and I regard the two of you as friends, so call on me if I can help you with anything in the future."

Chapter Seven

Anna climbs into her bed and turns off the lamp. What a long day this has been, but another happy one. This morning a judge declared the Dugans legal guardians of Hank and Bill. She whispers, "God, thank you for my blessings."

Carol stands at the bedroom door. "Anna, is it okay if I snuggle in your bed and talk for a little while? Then I'll go back to my room."

"Sure." She scoots over to make space for the little girl.

"I'm glad we have Danny, Hank, and Bill for brothers, but I miss special time with you."

"I know. I miss it too, but they need us. We're the only family they have. God wants us to share our love. When we're old women with walking canes, they'll still be our brothers."

Carol giggles. "They'll be old men when we're old women."

"That's right, but we'll still take care of each other."

"Anna, do you know that Bill will start kindergarten with me, but he doesn't know his ABC's. He knows most colors; he can count and write numbers, except he needs to know the alphabet."

"Let's start teaching him tomorrow. Hank needs assistance with English, although he's wise beyond his years in many things."

"Maybe Bart can help him."

"Bart's too busy trying to finish our house before the wedding on Friday afternoon, and his college classes start in two weeks. I'll ask Mary if she'll talk to Hank's principal and get some books for him."

"I can't help Hank, but I can help Bill—maybe. Do you think it'll be hard for him to learn to read because he talks like a-a hillbilly?"

"Carol!"

"He does. Like on cartoons. Danny doesn't, but Bill and Hank do. Mama scolds me if she hears me saying my words like that."

"They're smart boys. They'll learn and we have to be careful not to hurt their feelings. Eventually, they'll pronounce words correctly."

"Pro—what? I don't know that word."

"We'll talk about pronunciation tomorrow."

They are quiet for a few moments before Anna speaks. "Carol, while I cook breakfast in the morning, will you find some alphabet books? We'll play school tomorrow."

Bill wants to go with Bart, Danny, and Hank, to work on Bart and Anna's house. Anna tells him, "Bill, when you learn to say your ABC's, I'll drive you to where they're working."

He frowns but sits next to Carol. "Okay, show me what I need to learn. I know most of the letters; Grandma was helpin' me." Determined to go with the boys, he can say the alphabet before lunch.

Mary returns from the principal's office with a math book and a book Hank needs to read for class discussion. After supper, all four of the children sit in the sunroom doing homework that Anna assigns. Bart goes back to finish nailing the last of the molding in the master bedroom.

Mary comes to the kitchen for a cup of coffee and motions for Anna. She whispers. "If you and Bart are not going to your parents' farm on your honeymoon, do you mind if Charles and I take the kids down for the weekend? It should be an incentive for them to finish the books they're working on."

"Bart won't tell me where we're going, but he said nowhere near old memories. I think the kids would love going to the farm. Yesterday, I talked to Mr. Prince, and he said he still has six gentle mares in the pasture, so you can all ride."

Professor Dugan comes to the kitchen, and together they tell the children about the trip.

Danny jumps from his chair, pumps his arms and yells, "Yeah!"

Carol grins and slaps Danny's hand in a high five.

"Bill, you and Hank are gonna have fun. The week I stayed there was the most fun I've ever had, and we didn't even get to go swimming—it was too cold."

"Listen." Anna pauses until she has their attention. "That creek is fun, but it can turn into a demon after a heavy rain. If you see dark rain clouds upstream, get out of the water and rush to the house. Flash floods roar through that valley with a mighty fury."

They sit smiling as if she has told them a cute story. "I'm not kidding. You cannot escape the creek once a flash flood starts. The water is so swift that you will be miles downstream before it settles smoothly across fields. I almost drowned in a flash flood when I was eleven."

Carol stares with a worried frown. "How did you get out?"

"I was a good swimmer, but being a good swimmer won't save you—the water is too swift in a flash flood. A short distance downstream from where we swim, there is a rock ledge, with layers of rock going to the top of a hill—almost like a stairway. Dad showed it to me one winter day when there was no chance of getting snake bit. We climbed down to the ledge and back up."

"But how did that help you in the flood?"

"A willow tree grew near the ledge. I was lucky enough to grab onto a strong branch, pulling myself hand over hand until I got to the main part of the tree. Water was rising over the tree before I grabbed onto a rock, pulled myself onto the ledge, and climbed to the top of the hill. Later, another flash flood completely uprooted that willow and washed it away."

"That must have been scary," Carol says.

"Yes. I want you to remember it and leave the creek if you see rain approaching."

With somber faces, the children nod.

* * * * *

Friday afternoon, Professor Dugan waits with Anna, ready to walk her down the aisle. Mary sits on the front seat of the church auditorium. Hank and Bill escort guests to their seats, Danny stands beside Bart as best man. Carol, maid of honor, strolls toward the preacher. Anna's friend Jackie tends the guestbook.

Holding onto Professor Dugan's arm, Anna whispers, "I hope Mama and Daddy know what a wonderful family I've found."

The professor smiles. "They raised an amazing girl. We've been blessed to have you in our home."

On her way down the aisle, Anna pauses to hug Mary and

Bart's Aunt Alice. Later, after a supper prepared by the church women, Anna tosses her bouquet and runs to the car.

In the car she asks, "Now, will you tell me where you made reservations? I brought casual clothes, but I want to know where we're going."

"I rented a cabin beside a lake. It's near Heber Springs. Women from church packed an ice chest with enough food to last all weekend. I didn't tell anyone, except Aunt Alice, where we're going. She won't tell unless there is an urgent emergency."

She sighs and leans her head against his shoulder. "I love you, Bart."

"I love you." He leans to kiss the top of her head.

The western sky streaked with clouds resembling pink streamers meets blue skies as billows travel east. When Bart and Anna reach the secluded cabin, a gold moon reflects on the lake surface. They sit on the porch swing eating snacks prepared by Christian friends. An owl hoots in the distance and a fish splashes against the smooth surface of the lake.

Bart takes her in his arms, softly singing the words to "Unchained Melody."

* * * * *

In the morning, she wakes to the scent of coffee, and Bart's smiling face. He takes her hand, touching his lips to it. "Does my beautiful wife want a cup of coffee? Morning sun shines on the lake, and bluebirds replace last night's owl. The first day of our married life is magnificent."

Swinging her feet off the bed, she grabs his arm. "My head is still waltzing to your love songs."

He holds her against his chest and grabs a blanket from the bed. "Let's sit on the porch swing and have coffee, and then you can try my ham and cheese omelet."

She shivers and wraps herself in the blanket. "I wish we had a fire in the fireplace. It's cold this morning."

"Sit on the couch. We have kindling and wood." He strikes a match. Flames flicker and blaze into a warm fire.

"I've never been able to do that before."

He squints with a puzzled look. "Do what?"

She smiles. "Just wish and it happens."

With a grin, he bows. "Madam, your wish is my command."

"How about that ham and cheese omelet?"

He turns and quickly brings back a plate of omelet with strips of bacon and a buttered waffle. "My darling, your wish."

Taking the plate, she exclaims, "I like this kind of service."

"I'm not a bad cook."

"I can't beat this. From now on, you get to make our omelets. I love them, and mine get leathery on the edge before the middle gets done."

Anna turns on the radio while they wash dishes. The weatherman forecasts flash floods for most of Arkansas and the southern edge of Missouri. He warns that anyone in low-lying areas near a stream should move to higher ground.

"Bart, we're only a few feet from the lake. With all those hills and mountains above us we could be in danger."

He shakes his head. "I don't think so; that's a big lake. It would take a lot of rain to make it swell enough to put us in jeopardy."

"What if it washes away part of that narrow dirt road? We might have to walk out if that happens. We crossed a couple of shallow streams. Let's go home to our house. The Dugans were taking the kids to the farm for the weekend. Our little house will be as cozy as this."

He pulls her to her feet and kisses her forehead. "Okay, if that's your wish, fair lady."

In less than an hour, heavy rain is falling. Bart takes suitcases to the car and returns dripping wet. Anna in jean shorts and sandals runs to the car. She dries her hair, arms, and legs on a cotton sweater. "Turn on the heater. That rain is cold."

"It's August and we started the day with fire in the fireplace, now the heater."

"Who cares?" She snuggles against his arm. "Comfort is my goal."

He pushes the heater button.

The sky turns darker as they head south. "Bart, this weather makes me nervous. The water rises quickly in that creek and pours through the canyon with deadly force. I warned the kids to stay away from the creek if they see dark clouds in the distance."

"Did Mary and the professor hear you warning them?"

"I don't think so. They were in the den. Can we go by the farm? I have a terrible feeling that something bad is about to happen."

"Everyone will know we're going home."

"I don't care. They won't want to leave the farm."

He winks at her. "I'm afraid you're going to be worse than Aunt Alice to worry."

A weak smile combines with frown lines. "Aunt Alice kept you safe with her warnings. Those kids are so dear to me; I couldn't stand it if we lost one."

"We're on our way. We'll be there soon."

The closer they get to the farm, the more uneasy she becomes. "Hurry, Bart. Something is wrong. I feel it. Step on the gas. If you get a speeding ticket, I'll pay for it."

He chuckles. "Hey girl, we're married. What belongs to you belongs to me. So if you've got a pot of gold hidden away, half belongs to me."

"Okay, we'll pay it. Just hurry."

Before they reach the driveway, Anna sees the children in the field near the rock ledge. As Bart slows to a stop, she jumps from the car leaving her door open and runs half-climbing, half-jumping the fence. Bart follows close behind.

The younger boys, stand near the rolling water crying and slinging their hands. Hank climbs out of the creek and screams, "Carol's stuck in a thorn bush. I couldn't free her."

Holding to the rock ledge, Anna rushes into the water. Below the surface, Carol's limp body sways from the bush, her long blond hair tangled in thorny branches. Anna pulls and yanks clumps of hair and tugs at Carol's body, but the bush will not release its hold.

Bart, with a pocketknife, slices at Carol's hair and the bush until he pulls her free and to the surface.

Anna crawls onto the grass that is three inches deep in muddy water. "Lay her on my back and pump the water from her lungs." She turns her head sideways and rests on her folded hands with her nose above the water.

Bart plops Carol down on top of Anna and begins the rhythmical pumping to remove water from her lungs. Bill and Danny are on their knees praying, "Please, God. Please."

Hank kicks at the water. "It's not fair, God. It's not fair. Why do you keep takin' people we love?"

Anna yells, "Hank, run to my car, get my cell phone and call 911. Our road is Pony Lane. Tell them the Chapman farm."

At last, water gushes from Carol's mouth. After one more hard thrust against her back, Bart rolls her over, holds her nose, and with his mouth tight over hers, blows air into her lungs. He continues to work until she takes a breath, and then he carries her to the house.

Paramedics arrive, waking Mary and the professor from afternoon naps with loud sirens. They were unaware that the children went to the creek. Mary rides in the ambulance; Professor Dugan drives his SUV. Bart, Anna, and the boys follow in the car.

At the hospital, the doctor tells them that Carol will fully recover. "She may want to sleep a lot for a day or two, but after that, she'll return to normal."

When the doctor leaves, Professor Dugan asks, "Boys, can you tell me what happened?"

Danny folds his arms across his chest and steps close enough for Bart to put an arm around him. "Hank yelled, 'Rain's coming. Get out. Now!' Bill, Hank and I climbed the bank. I looked back at Carol just as she went underwater. She must have dropped something. Earlier, she said she forgot to take off the ring Anna gave her. Maybe that's what she was trying to get. The next thing I saw was a wall of water coming down the creek. Then I started praying."

Hank looks at Danny. "I saw her reach for that thorn bush and pull herself into it. I ran to the rocks next to it and went to her, holding to the rocks. Water covered her head, and she was tangled in the bush. I couldn't free her. I kept trying until I had to go up for air. That's when Anna and Bart came. I pulled and pulled but couldn't get her." His voice breaks into a sob, and he turns away.

Professor Dugan's voice hangs in his throat. "It took all of you to save her. The doctor says she'll recover, so let's hold hands and say a prayer of thanks."

Carol blinks. "Anna, I lost my ring."

"It's okay. A ring is replaceable; you are not." She smiles and reaches for Carol's hand.

After the prayer, Mary grabs Anna's shoulder. "What are you and Bart doing here? You are supposed to be on a honeymoon."

Bart answers, "We were in a secluded cabin beside the lake at Heber Springs. It's beautiful there, but when Anna heard the weather report, she got worried, and here we are."

Mary grasps Anna in a tight hug. "Thank God for guardian angels that whisper warnings and for sweet sisters and brothers."

Chapter Eight

Anna turns to look at the three boys in the back seat. Danny is asleep, his head against a window. In the middle, Bill leans against his brother, his eyes are closed, and his mouth is gaping. Hank stares out the left window, his black hair tousled, eyes squinting. "Anna, why does God keep throwing bad things at us? Why can't he let us be happy for a while?"

"Hank, I don't believe God sends bad things at us for no reason. Maybe he sends trials to strengthen us, but I believe bad things are from Satan."

"Everything I do seems to turn bad."

"What happened today wasn't your fault."

"I should have made sure all the kids got out of the water."

"Today was a lesson for Carol. She didn't heed your command. For a while after my parents died, I blamed myself for everything. Now, I realize there was nothing I could have done to prevent their death. As I study and understand more about God, I trust his love. No human is perfect, but God is. I hope you and Bill will go to church with us and learn about God's love."

"I'll go, but it'll take a lot of explaining to make me understand why Mama, Daddy, Grandma and Grandpa all had to die."

"The devil does bad things to make us doubt."

He turns in the seat and pulls Bill over so that his little brother looks more comfortable. "I've decided that I'm gonna try hard in school. Someday, I want to study engineering like Bart."

Anna smiles. "If you'll study, you'll be good at any profession you choose." Everyone is quiet for several minutes as the car travels along the interstate. "On Monday, if you want, we can go clean your Grandma's house and look for your Mama's things."

Hank frowns. "We may have to wait a while. I told Bart I'd help build a barn near your cabin. He told Bill and Danny they can get chickens if we get a place built where they can stay at night, safe from wild animals."

She stares at Bart. "Chickens! They'll poop all over the porches and my car."

"Not if we have a pen for them. Originally, they wanted to get horses or goats."

"Goats!" She wrinkles her nose. "Goats are hard to keep in a pen, and they stink."

"Horses are too expensive and they eat a lot of feed. We may have a hard time feeding ourselves until we graduate and find jobs."

"Maybe chickens are the best alternative, but I've seen hawks flying during the day and heard owls and coyotes in the night. 'Possum, skunks, raccoons, and bobcats roam these hills. Day or night, something is hungry for a chicken dinner."

"We'll build a strong pen with a wire top."

"All right, make sure you keep them off my car."

Bart grins and winks. "We're almost to Fayetteville. Are we going to our place or the Dugan house, and what are we going to eat? It's past lunchtime."

"We don't have food at our house, and I don't remember what is left in the ice chest. I know that Mary has cheese, chips, and oatmeal cookies, so we better stop there."

* * * * *

Bill crams the last bite of sandwich into his mouth. "I'm ready to go measure for that barn. We have some two-by-fours and lumber in the loft of Grandpa's barn. We can use that; can't we Hank?"

"Sure we can. The judge said everything that belonged to Grandpa and Grandma is ours."

Bart frowns. "I don't know about taking your stuff. What do you think Anna?"

"If the boys want to use it, why not? Otherwise, it may rot or get termites in it."

Hank leans on the table. "If there is enough of it maybe we can build a shed big enough for Grandpa's truck. I'm afraid someone will steal it if we leave it at the old house."

Anna drops a stack of paper plates on the counter. "That's a good idea. Let's build a pole barn. We have several cedars big enough for barn poles. I have Dad's chain saw to cut the poles. Maybe we could invite men from the church for a barn raising. I'll cook a big dinner for them. What do you think? We'll have an old-fashioned barn-raising party."

The boys grin and slap hands. "Yeah. That sounds like fun."

Bart's eyes widen. "We only have a week before school starts for the kids. We'll have to cut the poles this afternoon and plan the barn raising for next Saturday. Can you cook enough food by then?"

"I can, but the kids still have to do the homework I gave

them. I don't want anything to interfere with their education. Is that agreed?"

They all nod. "We'll do that after dark," Danny adds.

Bart jumps up from the table. "Anna, tell me where you stored that chainsaw. Boys, go put on your oldest, worn-out jeans and shirts. Wax from those cedar trees will ruin your clothes. Find some leather gloves to protect your hands. Anna, I noticed several in your Dad's toolbox—do you mind if they use those?"

She shakes her head. "They're my old ones, but they'll protect your hands. I never wore out leather gloves; several sizes are in there."

Bart slaps Danny on the back. "Timber, here we come."

Anna calls the preacher and asks if he will announce the barn raising and invite any man willing to lend a hand and any woman willing to help cook. She bakes four pies, two cakes, and ten dozen cookies and puts them in Mary's freezer before going to help Bart and the boys.

The hillside sounds like a lumber camp with the chainsaw buzzing and Hank chopping off branches with the axe. Danny and Bill drag cedar branches and dump them into a deep ditch to burn when it snows. Bill stops to sniff the air. "I love the smell of cedar—it reminds me of Christmas."

Danny inhales, "Yeah, but we need to add some oranges, apples and the scent of Grandma's homemade fudge. I could go for a handful of that."

Before sunset, fifteen tall poles, trimmed clean, lay scattered across the hillside. Hank wipes his brow on the back of his hand. "Tomorrow afternoon, we can get Grandpa's tractor from the shed and drag the poles to the barn location. Grandpa has an auger stored in the barn. If we can figure out how to use it, digging holes will be a lot easier."

Bart's eyes widen. "Wow, I didn't know you had a tractor. Does it have a front-end loader?"

"Yeah, it does. That tractor was Grandpa's pride and joy. He kept it in the shed covered with a big tarp. I need to go check on it and the truck. After Grandpa died, Grandma's drunken brother tried to talk her into letting him sell it. He'll steal it if he gets a chance.

Bart looks toward the low hanging sun. "Let's go now. We've got time before dark." He spreads a big towel over the truck seat to protect it from the tree wax on the boy's clothes.

"There's a kerosene soaked rag on that stump. Get it and wipe off as much cedar wax as you can. Soap and water will not cut that stuff. What the kerosene doesn't get will have to wear off. Bill, you have streaks of wax on both cheeks."

Bill giggles. "My face was itching, and I kept rubbing it with my sticky gloves."

Wearily, all five crowd into the truck and head toward Hank and Bill's old home. A dim light shines inside the house, and the tractor sits in the yard near the barn. Bart stops on the road and calls the sheriff.

"Deputies are on their way. Anna, do you still have that gun on your hip?"

"I do, and it's loaded. Snakes move about when the weather is hot. I came prepared for them, not a burglar."

Hank stretches his neck to see. "I bet it's our drunk uncle. He may have moved into the house."

With blue lights flashing, deputies pull into the yard. Within minutes, Uncle Al, handcuffed and staggering drunk, stumbles outside.

Hank requests that they search him. "Make sure he hasn't taken our mama's jewelry to pawn." His pockets contain a pearl necklace and a diamond ring.

The deputy hands the items to Hank. "Son, I suggest you search through the house and remove everything valuable. Store it somewhere safe. We'll take this guy to the county jail, but things have a way of disappearing from vacant houses."

"I'll do that sir. Thank you."

Anna goes with Hank to lock the doors. "It looks as if Uncle Al has spent several days in the house." Dirty skillets and grease cover the stove where he fried bear steak from the freezer. Empty whiskey bottles litter the counter top.

In Grandma's bedroom, Hank opens the chest and dresser drawers. In the closet, he finds an old suitcase. Inside are some of his mother's clothes and the pictures he wanted.

The doors locked, Hank puts the suitcase in Grandpa's truck. "Anna, do you think the Dugans will object to me parking Grandpa's truck and tractor in their backyard until we get the pole barn built?"

She shakes her head. "I don't think so. That should only take a week."

"Then do you mind driving the truck? I'll drive the tractor."

"I can do that. I'll go first and open the gate; the remote control is in my purse. You follow me. Bart, will you drive behind, in case one of us has a problem?"

"Don't run off and leave me. I'm so tired from running that chain saw, that I may fall asleep at the wheel."

"Danny, talk to Bart and keep him awake. Bill, I want you to ride in the truck with me."

With the vehicles parked in the Dugans' yard, Anna goes to

cook supper. Bart and the boys go for showers. Bacon, eggs, biscuits and gravy seem the quickest and easiest things to cook. She has it on the table when they come from the showers. "Boys, head for bed as soon as you finish eating. We're going to church in the morning. Tomorrow afternoon, you can work on the barn."

With his elbow on the table, Bart props his head on his hand. "Anna, we can't leave the boys here alone, and neither of our twin beds is big enough for both of us, so I'm gonna fall into that extra bed in the basement."

She grins. "Don't fall before you get there. I'll clean these dishes and go upstairs." She whispers in his ear, "We'll continue our honeymoon at the cabin when the Dugans come home."

Giving her a quick kiss, he leaves through the back door.

Watching until he enters the old rock garage, she sighs. "Fate spoiled the second day of the romantic weekend he had planned."

From the sunroom, she phones Mary, "How's Carol doing?"

"Fine. She finished a hamburger and fries; now she's working on a slice of chocolate cake. She wants to go home, but she'll have to wait until tomorrow. Charles went back to your farm, but I ordered a cot so I can sleep in the room with Carol." She laughs. "How is your romantic weekend with three young boys along?"

"We're at your house. Bart went to the basement with the boys. As soon as I put away supper dishes, I'll go upstairs. Don't worry; we're happy and have the rest of our lives for romantic weekends."

Sunday morning, Anna bakes cinnamon rolls, and fries ham

and eggs. Dressed for the church service, the boys rush in the back door. Bart says grace, leans back, and slowly rotates his head. "That chainsaw didn't do any favors for my neck and shoulders. I hope it feels better by this afternoon."

Anna heats a corn bag in the microwave and puts it on his neck. "Maybe this will help."

Rubbing his neck, he asks, "Do we have enough money to buy metal for the roof? No one has given us scrap tin."

"How much will it cost?"

"I'll check on prices first thing tomorrow morning."

"This afternoon, I'll have to buy concrete mix for setting the posts. If we don't have money for tin, we have problems. A little late, I've been thinking about Luke 14:28, where Jesus says if someone plans to build he sits down first and calculates the cost."

The boys excuse themselves to go brush their teeth.

"I didn't take the time to calculate."

"Bart, I don't know how much they will be worth, but while looking for Grandma's wedding dress, I found some stock certificates Mama and Daddy left for me."

He grins. "You do have a pot of gold hidden away."

"I doubt that."

"What kind of stocks are they?"

"I just glanced at them, but I remember they were big name companies. One is an aluminum company. I'll call Daddy's lawyer and ask him what I should do with them?"

"Aluminum is high dollar. Do you remember any others?"

She shakes her head. "I was planning for my wedding."

Slowly, he stands. "I need to shave and finish getting ready for church."

"Bart, I still have some gold left from that chest Carol and I found in the backyard."

He hugs her and kisses the top of her nose. "You are full of surprises. Do you have oil wells hidden away too?"

"No. Nothing else."

"If you have aluminum stock and gold bars, I'll not worry about the cost of a tin roof."

"It has to last until we graduate."

"It will, or I'll get a part-time job. Hey, put on your church dress. I'll bring the car around in twenty minutes."

Chapter Nine

Anna has breakfast waiting at daybreak on Saturday morning when Bart's engineering friends arrive at the barn site. They construct the frame with rafters in place and begin nailing two-by-fours across the top to hold the tin roof. Bart whispers to Anna, "We don't have enough two-by-fours. Should I call and have more delivered?"

She grips his hand, smiles and nods toward the road. A builder, from the church congregation, drives into the yard with a trailer full of two-by-fours—some are crooked, some are non-standard length, but they are good enough for barn building.

Bart ordered tin for the roof and sides but did not order enough to make doors. "I'll make sliding doors later. For now, the roof and sides will serve as a good garage."

In the late afternoon, the last piece of tin goes on. Men and boys move sawhorses under the shade and put plywood on top for tables. The women spread leftover food from the noon meal onto the improvised tables. Sitting on tailgates, cans, and boards, everyone enjoys an evening feast.

Someone opens a guitar case; an elderly man brings out a fiddle; Bill with a harmonica and Hank with his mandolin join to play bluegrass music. Soon people are singing. Anna taps her foot.

As darkness settles, the crowd dwindles. Mary instructs the boys and Carol to get in her car. "It's late, and we have Church tomorrow."

Bart holds Anna's hand and walks around admiring the new barn. A white moon lays a silver veil over the woodlands and night birds call softly from the shadows.

She stops to lean her head against his shoulder. "The sky is beautiful, but we were awake at four this morning preparing for workers. I'm exhausted."

They walk to the cabin and step onto the porch. "With all the work and excitement, I've never carried you over the threshold into our little house." Before she can comment, he sweeps her into his arms and walks inside. "Welcome home, sweetheart."

Sunday afternoon, Bart, Anna, Hank, and Danny gather scraps from the barn building and calculate how many sheets of tin they will need to build doors for the front and back of the barn. Carol and Bill spend the afternoon preparing for kindergarten.

Mary pre-registered the children in school and intended to take the morning and go with Carol and Bill to meet their teacher, but she must go to work and take care of an emergency. Anna volunteers to take them.

At the classroom, Miss Mayes, a first-year teacher, is nervous. Her co-teacher called in sick. "If you want, I'll stay and help," Anna says.

"Please do. I'll be very grateful."

The morning goes well until Miss Mayes assigns classroom monitors. Bill is the custodian of plants. Carol is in charge of the white mice, a hamster, and a guinea pig. Every child has a job that each will exchange for another at the end of the month.

One little girl tells the teacher that she does not want to be crayon monitor, "I want to take care of the animals."

"Maddi, next month you can care for the animals if you do a good job as crayon monitor. Everyone's job is important."

With a stubborn frown, Maddi breaks several crayons, dumps them in the guinea pig's water and opens the hamster cage allowing it to escape.

Bill offers sunflower seed to the hamster, catches and returns it to the cage. Maddi walks over and hits him in the stomach. "Leave my hamster alone."

Anna takes Maddi outside. "Do you like to swing? I'll push if you want."

"No. I hate swings and school. Mama sent me here to get rid of me. I hate her too."

Anna takes two peppermints from her pocket and offers one to Maddi. The little girl grabs the mint, angrily rips the paper off and sticks it in her mouth. "Give me the other one. I'm hungry. Mama pushed me out the door before I could eat."

Anna sits and places the second mint on the table before her. "Tell me about your mama."

With a shrug, Maddi begins. "Twila is her name. Granny named her that because she was born at twilight. She's not ugly. She's got long gold hair and lots of boyfriends. They love her, but they hate me and give me money to make me go away. They tell me to go to the store or the park." Again, she shrugs. "I don't care. I don't like them either."

"Do you have any brothers and sisters?"

"No. Mama said one kid is too many. She tried to get Granny to keep me, but she didn't want me 'cause Mama wouldn't let her have the food stamps and government money for keeping me. Nobody wants me 'cause I'm ugly and mean." She frowns and folds her fingers into fists.

"Who told you that you were ugly?"

"Granny and some of Mama's boyfriends."

"Maybe that's because you were acting ugly, but you have beautiful smoky blue eyes, and your hair would be pretty if we brush it." Anna takes a small plastic brush with a folding handle from her pocket. "Will you let me brush your hair? I'll take extra care and try my best not to pull."

Maddi does not say a word, but scoots close. With the little brush, Anna starts at the bottom of Maddi's dark hair and works her way gently through it until all the tangles are gone. She parts and braids it, fastening the ends with rubber bands from her pocket. "Now, you are truly beautiful."

As Anna brushed, the little girl told the sad story of her home life. Anna wishes she could take her home, teach God's love, and show her the way a loving family lives.

"Maddi, at lunchtime, will you sit with me and be my friend?"

Maddi nods and reaches to stroke the braids. "I've never had braids."

After school, Carol and Bill tell Mary about Maddi. "Bill, I'm proud of you for not hitting her. The teacher will take care of that little girl."

"Grandpa told me never to hit a girl."

Anna hears Carol whisper to Bill, "If she hits you again, I'll bust her nose. Maddi's a brat."

"Carol, I want to read you something from the Bible." She opens her Bible and reads from Matthew 5:39, where Jesus says, "If someone strikes you on the right cheek, turn to him the other also."

Carol looks down at her hands without immediate comment.

Bill and Carol report that Maddi picks on a different child every day. The children back away, and try to keep their distance.

On Friday afternoon, Anna goes to help in the classroom and sees Maddi slap Carol for no apparent reason. Carol responds in a low voice, "Jesus said, 'Turn the other cheek.'" Maddi grins and slaps her hard on the right cheek.

Quick as a flash, Carol hits Maddi on the nose with her fist. "I don't have another cheek, and I'm tired of you picking on kids. If you want, I'll be your friend, or do you want an enemy to hit you every time you hit one of my friends?"

Maddi stands, looking at the floor where blood drips from her nose. Anna, helping a group of children write the alphabet, pretends not to see, but glances up as the teacher goes to Maddi.

"What happened, Maddi?" She holds a wad of tissues to the child's nose. "Go stand over the bathroom sink. I'll bring you some ice."

Maddi goes to the sink without answering the teacher's question. Carol wipes blood from the floor with a paper towel before going to her seat. The other children stare—no one tattles.

Anna notices that Maddi's hair was not brushed before school. She has on the same dirty clothes she wore yesterday when Anna came for Carol and Bill. At snack time, Maddi is first to the table and grabs two graham crackers and extra fruit.

After school, Anna tells Bill and Carol to wait outside while she speaks with the teacher. Miss Mayes is equally concerned for Maddi. "Yesterday, she waited outside the classroom until almost dark for her mother. I didn't see the woman come to get her, and I didn't see her drop Maddi off this morning. I'm wondering if I should call the police or Child Services."

"Maddi needs a home with someone to love her. If you don't care, I'll call Mrs. Dugan. She knows the Child Services director. Maybe she can discover something fast." While they wait, Anna brings Carol, Bill and Maddi inside for a snack. Mary, already approved as a foster parent, receives permission to take Maddi home until her mother is located.

A neighbor tells a social worker from Child Services that, "Two days ago, Maddi's mama packed bags into her boyfriend's car and left. I watched Maddi walking home near dark, and saw her crawl through a bedroom window to get in the apartment. I guess, I should have called someone, but I try to mind my own business."

Anna takes Maddi home with the other children and prepares supper for the family. "Carol, get you and Maddi some clean pajamas so that you can take your baths. It will be dark soon, and Mary has had a hard day. After we eat, I'll read you a story before Bart and I go home. Carol, you use your mama's bathroom. I'll get Maddi a towel, some shampoo and show her where to bathe."

A week passes and Child Services or the police have not located Maddi's mama. A judge gives the Dugans temporary custody. Carol treats Maddi with as much love as Bill, Hank, and Danny.

After the first day, Maddi never argues and quickly learns household rules from the other children. She is the same size as Carol, and Carol enjoys sharing, but Mary orders a complete wardrobe for Maddi. With the new outfits comes a Barbie doll and Barbie clothes.

Maddi hugs Mary and exclaims, "I've never had a Barbie.

One of Mama's boyfriends got mad and pulled the head off the baby doll a neighbor gave me. I tried to tape the head back on, but Mama threw it in the trash."

Tears fill Mary's eyes as she hugs Maddi and strokes her long black hair.

Maddi settles into Anna's old room and keeps it neat. She and Carol play together and rarely quarrel. Anna is surprised to learn that Maddi can read. "I listened as Granny's neighbor taught her little girl. Leigh had a crippled foot, so her mama taught her at home. Leigh helped me read until they moved away."

* * * * *

The pecan trees in the Dugans' yard hang heavy with nuts. They start falling in October. Danny asks Professor Dugan if the kids can gather and sell them at the Farmers Market. "We need computers for homework, especially me and Hank. If we sell the pecans, we might get enough to buy a couple. Bill, Carol, and Maddi don't have homework in kindergarten. They can get something else with their share."

"That's a good idea, Danny. I'll park my old truck under a tree and you boys can load it. I doubt that Carol and Maddi will want to help."

The boys gather nuts under one tree, park the truck underneath and spread old tarps, and sheets of plastic under the other trees. Danny and Hank climb into the trees and shake the lower branches. Pecans thump against the plastic with each quiver of a limb.

Midweek a strong wind blows from the west. Thursday and Friday after school, the boys empty the tarps into buckets and sacks. Saturday, Professor Dugan drives the packed truck to the Farmers Market. They sell all the pecans.

That night, they count the money, shout and slam hands together. The sales came to almost four hundred dollars. Danny slaps Hank on the back, "We haven't collected half of them yet. We may have enough to buy a computer for Bill."

Bill smiles. "I hope so; I need to start learning if I'm going to be as smart as you two."

They sell all the pecans and earn enough money to buy two computers with programs and a printer. Hank sets up his grandpa's old computer for Bill. The computer sets Bill on a quest for knowledge.

Anna registers for enough classes to meet her scholarship requirements and still have time to help Mary take care of the children in the afternoon. She picks the kids up from school and helps with homework while she cooks supper. Bart stops by long enough to eat and is off to another class.

She has one class with her friend Jackie but never sees her outside class. Jason, Jackie's old boyfriend, has a new girlfriend. He has one class with Bart.

* * * * *

As Thanksgiving approaches, Bart makes plans to work on doors for the barn, but the weather turns extremely cold. On Tuesday afternoon, Bart brings in an armload of wood for the wood heater and dumps it into the wood box. "Anna, I think I'll wait on those doors until spring unless it turns warm for Christmas break. I chained Hank's tractor to one of the barn poles, and his truck to another. A thief would have a hard time stealing either one."

"I agree. If you and the boys work outside in this weather, you might get sick and miss classes. The barn works well enough as a shed." She tosses another stick of wood into the stove.

"Professor Dugan wants to buy wire to fence the family land—Carol's, ours, and Hank and Bill's. Did he talk to you about that?"

"No, but I can't possibly help unless we do it at one of the long breaks or wait until summer. I'm under pressure with school this semester."

"We know that. I think he wants to do it during spring break. Then we can turn the horses into the pasture for summer. Mary's tired of them being in the backyard."

"I can understand that. It wasn't so bad with Polka, but two horses are too much. I'm surprised neighbors haven't complained."

"They probably would if Hank and Danny didn't keep the yard clean."

"Hank has been worrying about his grandpa's tools, especially the auger and brush hog. Can you store the small tools in the garage and chain the auger and brush hog in the barn?"

"We can do that over the Thanksgiving weekend."

Anna nods. "Today after school, I'll help the boys move the small tools to the old garage behind the Dugans' house."

After Hank tells the professor that he is worried about someone stealing the tools, Professor Dugan instructs him to load them into his old fishing truck. Yesterday, Hank and Bill saw fresh footprints around the barn. Uncle Al is no longer in jail and is probably looking for something to pawn for whiskey money.

"I'd help, but I have a class. Let Hank lift the heavy tools—he's strong. Have you noticed how his arms and shoulders are developing?"

"Yes, and Danny and Bill are filling out—not fat, just muscle. For a while, I was worried about Bill—he was too thin."

"Hank keeps them busy. If they're not building something, they're tilling a garden for next spring, racing, climbing, or playing ball." He opens a heavy book. "Hon, you don't have to wait up. Go to bed where you can stay warm. I have several long chapters to read before class tomorrow."

"I'll keep wood in the stove for a while. I also have chapters to read." Anna sits in the rocker, holding her book, and stares through the stove's glass door at red-orange flames dancing over split wood.

After school the following day, Anna and the children climb into Professor Dugan's truck and go to load tools. Someone has been in the barn. "Anna, some of the most expensive machinist tools are missing. Grandpa had some micrometers and other precision tools." Hank kicks a barn post. "If the police catch him, I want to press charges. He's a sorry low-down thief."

"Hank, do you know why your uncle started drinking in the first place?"

"I think it's a trait that's inherited. Grandma said some Indians can't stay away from it after they take a drink or two. She said it's the same with drugs. Bill and I swore not to try drugs or liquor. I'd hate for anyone to think I'm as disgusting as Uncle Al. Grandma said he was gentle and kindhearted before he began drinking. Alcohol made a demon of him."

"Has he ever tried to stop?"

"He's been in the VA Hospital several times, but he always

goes back to whiskey or cheap wine when he's almost broke."

"Has he ever gone to AA?"

"I don't know. It seems that he doesn't care enough to try his best, but Grandma said he's had a hard life, and he's trying to forget."

"I'll check with someone at AA and see if they can get someone to meet with him."

"Do what you want; I don't care. I wish they'd lock him in jail and keep him."

With the tools loaded, Hank wants to check inside the house. A skillet is scorching on the stove. Uncle Al is asleep on the couch with an empty bottle in his hand. Hank calls the sheriff. Another pawn ticket taken from the old man's pocket proves that he pawned the tools.

The sheriff slaps Hank on the back. "Son, I'd tell you to change the locks, but a drunk would break a window to get inside. I don't know a solution to your problem, other than locking him up permanently, and he'll have to be charged with a serious crime for us to do that."

"Breaking, entering, and theft of property is not serious enough?"

"He had a key and claimed your grandma gave it to him."

Chapter Ten

On the phone, a man from AA promises Anna that he will go to the jail, talk to Uncle Al, and try to get him in an apartment.

Hank frowns and closes a book he is reading. "Did you ask if they could get him one in Mexico or somewhere far away?"

"No, Hank. As Christians, we're obligated to help him."

"I don't understand that. He broke into our house and stole from us. I wish they would keep him in jail."

Saturday, Professor Dugan follows Hank as he goes to move the brush hog. Hank does not need help; he has assisted his Grandpa with the equipment. "Sir, I'd like to run the brush hog over the level fields until near dark."

"Hank, is it legal for a fourteen-year-old boy to drive a tractor with a brush hog?"

"I've done it many times for Grandpa. As far as I know, you don't have to have a license to drive a tractor on your land. It's not dangerous unless I run into a hole or ditch, run under a tree limb and get pulled off, or do some other stupid thing. I'm careful. Tell the other kids to stay inside when I come near the house. The blades might sling a stick or limb into the yard."

"I'll do that, but be cautious. Farm equipment makes me nervous. I've always been a city boy."

Before dark, Hank clears the level ground close to the Dugan home and goes over a few acres near Bart and Anna's little house. He pulls the tractor under the pole barn roof and chains it to one of the poles. After removing the key, he knocks on Anna's door. She is still at the Dugans' and Bart is away, working on a project with his engineering friends.

He walks across the field toward the gate. As he nears the rock wall, Curly barks. "Curly, get someone to open the gate." The little dog barks harder and Hank yells. At last, Anna hears him yelling and opens the big steel gate.

Back inside, Anna calls, "Professor, dinner's ready."

"I've got to go get Hank. I fell asleep in my recliner and forgot about him." Half asleep, he stumbles toward the garage.

"Professor, Hank's here. He walked home. He's in the bathroom washing his hands."

Hank steps into the kitchen with a grin. "I cleared Carol's land and part of Anna's. It looks a lot better without brush and weeds."

"I'm sorry, son. That recliner took me away. I'm glad you didn't have an emergency while I was sleeping."

"Me too, but while I was walking, I noticed a guy farther down the road toward Grandma's house. I couldn't tell what he looked like, but he ducked into the bushes when he saw me. Why would a guy do that?"

The professor frowns. "I don't know. It's rare for anyone to use that road. Your granny's house and Bart and Anna's are the only houses that front on it. Maybe someone was hiking."

"But why would they hide?"

"I don't have an answer for that. Could it be your Uncle Al?"

"No. He walked like a young man. It wasn't Uncle Al. He's still in jail—unless that guy from AA bailed him out."

After dinner, Professor Dugan turns on the news. Anna,

walking past the den, hears the announcer say that a young man escaped from the county jail after an arrest on drug-related charges. They believe he is wearing jeans and a yellow shirt, stolen from a clothesline near the jail. An enlarged picture appears on the screen. She draws in her breath. "I've seen that guy before. He was Jaeger's friend, maybe a cousin. Everyone I know that was friends with Jaeger is a low-life."

Hank says, "Professor Dugan, that guy I saw on the road wore jeans and a yellow shirt, but this is a long way from the county jail."

"Someone might have given him a ride."

"I don't think Anna should go home by herself tonight. If you let me have Grandpa's rifle, I'll go stay with her until Bart comes home."

"I'll call the sheriff and ask him to look along that road and Bart can pick Anna up here."

"It may be ten or eleven before he leaves his study group."

"I'm sure Anna wouldn't sleep until he gets home. She may as well wait here. I'll stay awake and read—I had a nap. You need your rest, so you can remain alert in church tomorrow."

The sheriff sends deputies to check along the road but does not find anyone.

At breakfast, Professor Dugan comments, "I didn't expect the sheriff to find that guy. There are too many ravines, bushes and trees to conceal someone wanting to hide. I think you kids should stay inside the yard this afternoon. Don't take the horses into the fields."

Monday morning, the local news station warns people to remain on the lookout for a man about six feet tall, with dark brown hair and brown eyes. His picture flashes on the screen again. He may be armed and should be considered dangerous.

Anna puts breakfast dishes in the dishwasher and calls the children to get in the car. Mary, Professor Dugan, and Bart are already gone.

Carol and Maddi calmly skip into the kitchen. Suddenly, Carol clasps her hands and yells, "My reader!" She runs through the house, frantically looking for her new book. "I don't remember where I put it, and I'll get a bad grade if I don't bring it back." Bill and Maddi help her look, but they cannot find it.

"Maybe Mama accidentally mixed it with her papers. I'll call her." Mary does not have the book; neither does Professor Dugan. Bart always turns his phone off when he leaves for school.

Hank is getting aggravated. "Carol, I have a test the first period. We have to go. Maybe it's still in the car. Did you read it last night or at all over the weekend?"

"No, I didn't." She and Maddi run for the car while Anna locks the doors and checks the stove burners.

Danny grabs Anna's arm. "That guy's in the garage and Carol and Maddi are out there. I saw his yellow shirt. Call 911."

She hands him her phone. "You do it, and then stay in here. You too, Hank." She runs upstairs, takes the professor's pistol from a high shelf in his bedroom. She found the gun last week while cleaning.

After unlocking the door to the basement stairwell, she tiptoes down. Glad that recently she oiled the locks, she turns the deadbolt for the rock hallway—it does not squeak.

The walkway to the garage is dark, except for thin splinters of light that filter through the cracked wall as she slips toward the garage. Anna hears a man say, "Keep quiet."

Carol wails, "I'm sick, I'm gonna throw up, let me outside."

"Hush."

Carol gags and sprays vomit onto the garage floor. The man moves back, swearing in a low voice as she slides from the car and runs choking and wheezing toward the outside. With his attention focused on Carol, Maddi kicks both feet against the partly open car door; it hits and knocks him off balance. He grabs for the stair rail, dropping his gun. The gun bounces over the stairway to the basement floor, as Maddi dashes outside to check on Carol.

Anna runs forward. "Hold it. Stand still or I'll shoot."

"That little brat puked on my shoes."

Anna frowns. "You'll fit in with the drunks in jail."

"You're a real comedian."

"What are you doing here?"

Turning a shoe left and right, he ignores her question. "I need a paper towel from that roll on the wall. I've got to get this puke off."

"All right, but no quick moves." As he comes down the stairs, Anna steps back onto a small chunk of cement and turns her ankle. "Oh!" She cries.

He lunges to grab the gun but steps on the teeth of a rake someone left on the floor. The rake handle pops up and hits him in the face. His lip drips blood and a knot puffs above his eyebrow.

Anna holds her gun until police officers arrive and take him away. "I wonder how many more of Jaeger's old friends want to kill me bad enough to come looking."

Detective Miller pats her shoulder. "I want you to go over some mug shots and try to identify anyone you remember talking with Jaeger. Then we'll keep an eye on them."

"I think that guy's related to Jaeger's mama, maybe her nephew."

He shakes his head. "I hope there's not a big clan of Jaeger's family."

"I worry more about these kids, but I'm not eager to die."

"They're not after the kids."

"I've got to stay alert."

Detective Miller grins. "Anna, at night when you say your prayers, don't you ask God to watch over you and the children, and keep you safe?"

"Yes, every night."

"Matthew 7:7 says *Ask and it will be given to you* . . . . God answered your prayers."

"Yes, He did and I'm thankful.

"Thanksgiving is next week. That'll give me a few days to stay off this sprained ankle."

"Carol and the other kids will have to take care of you for a while."

"Carol is probably getting tired of being my nurse. She's been helping me since I got out of the hospital after Jaeger's beating."

"Hank wants you to teach him how to cook. That could be an opportunity for him to learn and help you as well."

Chapter Eleven

Anna misses one day of class because of her ankle injury. Thanksgiving morning, she sits in a chair helping Mary peel and mix. Professor Dugan rakes the front yard while waiting for dinner. Hank left early with his tractor and brush hog to clear more of the family fields. Bart works on a project with his engineering friends. Carol, Maddi, Danny and Bill take turns riding the horses. They are all doing things they love.

Anna stares out the window at the children. "Mary, sometimes I wonder if I'm dreaming that I've found such a wonderful family. Then, someone from Jaeger's family comes along and makes me realize that not everything is wonderful. I go from being so happy I could dance, to being depressed, but I know God watches over me."

Mary bends to hug her. "We just have to pray and trust in God. I truly believe that He has something extraordinary planned for you and Bart. I've never seen a young couple more kind and caring for others. The children adore you."

"Bart is unique. He's been my protector since I was a little girl."

"I knew you were special the first day I met you. Carol was becoming a problem child before you came to stay with us. Until that day, she would never talk to strangers but she accepted you instantly. The change you enacted was near magic."

Anna smiles. "That's a wonderful compliment."

"I mean every word of it. You are special. The problems you keep facing may occur as trials to prepare you for something. The life God has planned may not transpire as easy, but I'm sure you can handle it."

Anna shivers. "I hope it's not worse than my life with Jaeger."

"It may be a wonderful life. Maybe you've already faced the worst of your trials."

Anna sits quietly for several minutes. "Mary, what could God have planned for Bart and me?"

Mary's hand stirs a pot faster. "Oh dear, my feeble brain can't possibly fathom God's plans. He may want the two of you to become missionaries. You will be an exceptional teacher for children or adults when you complete your education—so will Bart, and he'll have an engineering degree. Engineering knowledge is priceless in undeveloped countries."

Deep in thought, Anna frowns. "Mary, please don't tell Bart about our conversation. He has so much on his mind lately, and I don't want to add to it. If God has a special plan for us, He'll reveal it at the right time."

The phone rings. Anna looks at the caller ID and lifts the receiver. "Good morning, Detective Miller. Yes, the cooking class is still in our plans. The kids are looking forward to it."

Mary reaches for the phone. "Detective, this is Mary. If you don't have plans for dinner, come celebrate with us. We have a twenty-pound turkey in the oven and need someone to share it. You've been around so much the past year that we've adopted you into our family. Hold on a minute. I have to turn off a burner."

She lifts the phone again. "Charles is trying to stay busy and away from the kitchen. He raked leaves, and now, he's gathering tools to go over to Hank's grandma's and winterize the house before that storm comes in to freeze the pipes. If you know anything about winterizing a house, please come give them advice."

She places the phone in the cradle. "I'm glad he called. I meant to invite him yesterday. I don't think he has family in Arkansas. It wouldn't be Christian to let him eat alone."

"Mary, I don't know of anything else I can do to help. Do you mind if I go with them to shut off the water and get it ready for winter? I used to help Dad do that to a neighbor's house when they went away."

"By all means. Go with them, and tell Charles what they need to take."

"They'll need anti-freeze, the kind people use in campers."

Mary shouts from the garage door, "Charles, can you come in here and listen to Anna? She's helped winterize a house." Leaving the door open, she runs back to the stove.

Professor Dugan steps inside. "Anna, I wish you didn't have a sprained ankle so that you could go with us. I've never done this and don't know where to start."

"I can go if you'll park close to the kitchen door, so I don't have to limp across the yard. Dad always bought pink anti-freeze from a camper dealership to pour in the toilets and drains. They'll tell you what to buy."

He looks at his watch. "I better go now. They'll close at noon. Ride over to the house with the boys and get them started on draining the water."

Detective Miller arrives shortly after the professor leaves.

"My, your house smells good. Is there anything I can do to help—maybe taste a few things?"

Mary laughs and points toward the sunroom. "Anna made appetizers. Help yourself."

Anna is putting on heavy wool socks. "Good morning, Detective Miller. My ankle may hurt worse if it gets cold, but I need to get outside. I'm a country girl and don't enjoy being confined inside for long periods."

"I brought my air compressor to blow the excess water out of the lines. That way we don't need to put anti-freeze in the hot water tank, and you won't have that awful chemical taste in the water when you turn it on in the spring."

From the kitchen, Mary joins in the conversation. "It's a good thing you and Anna know what to do. Charles was going to turn the water off at the road and turn it on in the house to drain."

"We'll need to do that and drain the hot water tank, but we need to blow the excess water out so it can't freeze in low places and break the lines."

Hank comes inside with Bill and Danny. "Anna, I'll bring my truck around and back it close to the garage. I've already loaded plumbing tools."

"Detective Miller, do you mind taking Danny and Bill?"

"Glad to have them. Boys, my truck's out front."

At his grandma's house, Hank unlocks the kitchen door and slams his hand against the cabinet. "Uncle Al's been here again, and he didn't wash the skillet and clean up the grease. We've got to find a way to keep him out before he burns the house."

Everyone follows Hank into the living room. "He even built a fire in the fireplace and left without covering it or putting up the screen."

Anna shivers and pulls her coat tighter. "We'll cover it when we leave. Toss some more wood on and get it warm in here."

With a heavy sigh, Hank turns. "I'll get an armload." He steps into the hall and stops. "They used to have a floor furnace here, but grandpa thought it used too much gas. When something went wrong with it, he removed the heater. Grandma always covered the grate with that—" He pauses to point. "That heavy rug. I wonder why Uncle Al took it off. Grandma used to send Bill and me under the house through this hole when she thought a tornado was near."

He lifts the heavy grate. A small dark head, with wide brown eyes, appears. "Bill, what are you doing under the house?"

Standing behind him, Bill answers, "That's not me, but he's kinda like looking in the mirror. What's your name kid?"

The boy ducks his head and disappears. Hank runs outside and returns holding a squirming, squealing child, tight in his arms. "I caught him as he tried to come out from under the house."

"Let him go. We were only trying to keep warm." A beautiful dark haired woman is on her knees inside the hole that once held the floor furnace.

"This is our house." Hank frowns. "How did you know that no one was living here?"

Looking as if she might cry, she rubs a hand over her eyes. "I didn't. When I was evicted from my apartment, I figured Aunt Lou would let us stay with her for a while, but my car ran out of gas about a mile down the road. I didn't have money to buy more gas, so we walked here. We were almost frozen, and it was getting dark. No one answered our knock, but I remembered playing under the house as a kid, so we crawled underneath to get out of the cold wind."

"So you knew about this hole in the floor."

"No. Curt bumped against the grate and discovered we could get into the house through it. We haven't taken anything but a little wood and some meat from the freezer. I'll pay for it when I get a job, but we're in a bad shape now—there's not a nickel in my purse." She raises her head to scan the faces watching her. "Did Aunt Lou move away?"

Hank stares with a deep frown. "She died. I'm Hank Bird. Henry Bird was my dad. Who are you?"

"Aunt Lou's dead!" A sob catches in her throat. "She was my last hope." The young woman covers her face with her left hand and digs the fingers of her right hand into her side as she hugs herself.

She takes a deep breath and begins, "I'm Joann. Your Uncle Al is my dad, but I was little when Mama left Daddy for the last time. He couldn't keep a job, was always drunk and beating on Mama. When I was ten, I stayed a week here with Aunt Lou. Mama needed surgery and didn't have anyone to keep me. That's when Aunt Lou told me to come to her if I needed help. That was years ago."

"Grandma told me about you and showed me the picture you sent last year." Hank looks toward Professor Dugan, standing in the kitchen holding two jugs of pink anti-freeze. "What should we do, Uncle Charles?"

"We'll talk about it after we eat. Let's get this house good and warm and leave the water dripping while we go home for Thanksgiving dinner. After we demolish that turkey, we'll decide what to do about winterizing."

Professor Dugan introduces himself to Joann and Curt.

"Joann, I insist that you and your son come home with us for dinner. My wife had a big turkey in the oven when we left."

She looks down at her clothes—dirty from crawling underneath the house. "That sounds good, but . . . ."

Stepping closer, Anna says, "You have to come. We have enough food cooked to feed two big families. Don't worry about your clothes. You can take a hot shower while I help Mary set the table."

Danny has added an armload of dry wood to the fireplace. Flames dance over the wood, crackling softly as the room fills with warmth. Bill and Curt stare at one another. Bill says, "You'd look like my twin if you were a little bigger."

"Or if you were a little smaller." Curt grins.

Anna limps toward the kitchen. "Joann, gather whatever you need to take with you while I set all the faucets to dripping. They need to dribble enough to keep them from freezing. Afterward, we'll go get gas for your car and bring it here before some thief strips it."

Detective Miller motions to her. "I've got a can in my truck. Come with me and I'll get you to a station and back here within a short time."

Joann pats at her hair, avoiding eye contact. "I don't have money to pay for gas."

"Don't worry." Detective Miller shrugs. "I need to pay forward for blessings I've received. I'll fill your car. Come on Curt, you can help me and your mama."

Anna hobbles around setting all the faucets to a slow drip. Professor Dugan covers the fire with ashes. Hank and Danny go outside to close all the vents and the door to the crawl space. Bill washes the greasy skillet left on the stove and wipes the kitchen cabinet. With everything secure, they meet outside as Detective Miller stops on the road, and Joann pulls her car under the carport.

Swinging his arm Professor Dugan yells, "Let's go check on dinner."

At the Dugan house, Anna shows Joann where she can shower before returning to help Mary with last minute dinner preparations. Detective Miller is on the floor helping Danny, Bill and Curt build a domino train. Curt sits close to him.

Professor Dugan sets the turkey on one end of the table. "Everyone grab a dish of food and bring it to the table. I'm hungry."

"Pies and cake stay on the counter until later," Mary announces.

Maddi and Carol walk beside the cabinet. Maddi leans close to a cake. "I want a slice of this coconut cake."

"So do I," Carol says, "With chocolate sauce poured over it. Coconut is Bart's favorite. Anna made that for him, but she said he has to share."

Bart crosses the kitchen from the back door. "No, Carol, Anna said that's all mine."

They grin at each other. "You'll have to fight me and Maddi. We get the first servings."

Detective Miller holds a chair for Joann, but Curt slides into it. Moving over two chairs, he motions for Joann and then sits between them. The children fidget until Professor Dugan says grace and the food is passed around the table. For several minutes, forks touching plates make the only sounds in the room.

Joann is the first to speak. "I didn't dream we would have

such a wonderful dinner. I'm truly thankful for your hospitality."

Hank places his fork on his plate and looks at Joann. "We decided that you and Curt can stay in Grandma's house until you find a job if you promise to be careful with the fireplace. I'd hate for Grandma's house to burn."

"We'll be careful. When I find a job, I'll pay the rent." She lowers her head. "I think DHS will help us now that we have an address. I was afraid to ask them before—afraid they would take Curt from me because we were homeless."

Detective Miller turns to Joann, "I'll take you to DHS on Monday, and we can go to the Unemployment Office. What kind of work are you looking for?"

"I have receptionist experience. In high school, I worked in the office. I could type sixty-five words per minute. I'd like to get an office job."

"I'll ask around and let you know if I hear of anything open."

Anna snaps her fingers. "My friend Jackie works at the mall. She said there was a job opening in an insurance office a few doors down from her. The mall is open tomorrow if you want to check on that."

"Yes, I do want to check on it. Is it close enough for me to walk?"

"No, but Doug filled your car with gas."

"Thank you. You are all kind." She turns to look at Detective Miller. "And Mr. Miller, I appreciate your help with my car."

He grins. "Why don't you call me Doug?"

She blushes. "I'll do that."

Carol slides from her chair. "Is anyone ready for dessert? Maddi and I want cake."

Curt looks at his plate with a frown. "I took too much turkey."

Detective Miller whispers to him. Curt grins and nods. Doug sticks his fork into the slice of meat on Curt's plate. "Carol, will you put this in Curly's bowl?"

She nods and takes the fork from his hand. "Do you want coconut or chocolate cake, or pumpkin pie?"

Detective Miller says, "Chocolate cake without the sauce while I help myself to a cup of black coffee. Joann, do you and Curt want coffee?"

Curt giggles, "I want chocolate cake, but no coffee. I have milk."

Joann stares at Doug's eyes. "Yes, black coffee, please."

While pouring her coffee he asks, "Tomorrow morning, would you like me to drive you to the mall? We might discover some other places where you can apply, and eat lunch while we're looking."

Anna smiles at Bart, and he winks as they walk to the kitchen with plates. "We finished our engineering project. We'll turn it in next week. Tomorrow I can spend the day with my sweet wife."

She laughs and whispers. "We have six children to entertain tomorrow. Mary has to work, Professor Dugan is preparing a lesson plan for his class, and Joann is going to check on a job with that insurance agent in the mall."

"Six! How will we entertain them when it's too cold to play outside?"

"We planned a cooking class, but Detective Miller promised to drive Joann. So, in the morning, we'll sort and do laundry. After lunch, we'll go to the movies. Mary said it is her treat."

He frowns and turns to the boys, gathered around the desserts. "Hank and Danny, if I can talk Anna into doing our laundry, will you two help me work on doors for the barn?"

They nod. "Sure thing. Building is fun," Danny adds, "Yeah, and I hate doing laundry."

Bill, Carol, Maddi, and Curt look at each other. Carol shrugs. "Your hands will freeze to the hammer. I'd rather wash clothes."

Chapter Twelve

Sunday, Detective Miller takes Joann and Curt to church and lunch. That afternoon, he splits firewood for the fireplace. Curt and Joann stack it on the porch where it will stay dry.

Monday morning, Joann takes Curt to a day care facility and begins work in an insurance office. Detective Miller stocks the house with groceries for Joann and Curt and eats with them every night that he is not working.

A week later, Bart and Anna sit near the wood heater in their little house sipping hot chocolate. The only sound inside is the soft crackle of the fire. "Bart, I love every one of those kids, but our little house is a peaceful oasis after a noisy day with them. Carol and Maddi are best friends; they never fight, but giggle constantly. Bill has accepted Curt as his little brother and continually shields him from trouble."

Bart nods and smiles. "Hank and Danny are big buddies. Danny acts as if Hank knows everything. Although Danny excels in some things, Hank is world wise. They help each other and never gloat over things they know. Working with them is a joy. We've almost finished the barn doors. Next Saturday, if the weather is good, we may get them hung, and the rest of the barn enclosed."

"I'm glad the barn is almost finished so that we can store our tools. In one corner, let's pour a concrete floor for a tool room and use the plywood those builders gave us to enclose it."

"We'll need to get it poured before we install the doors."

"Mary is still paying me to take care of Carol and the children. Last week I got a bonus." She grins. "Your frugal wife saved most of it; we can use that for cement and not take money from our savings."

He stands and pulls her into his arms giving her a gentle kiss. "I love you, frugal wife."

Detective Miller's truck roars by on the road. Anna leans her head against Bart's chest. "You can set your clock by him. Every night at nine, he's on his way home. Have you noticed how awe-struck he is with Joann? His face seems to glow when she walks into the room."

"I've noticed, and Curt is crazy about him, but I don't see that sparkle in her eyes. She respects him, but I don't think she's falling in love. I wish I could warn him, but I don't know how."

Anna sighs. "Neither do I. He's not exactly handsome, although she couldn't find a nicer guy to be a daddy for Curt. She might learn to love him, but she's beautiful and through the years will have men flirting with her. I can only imagine how Detective Miller will react to that."

"Not well, I'm afraid. Do you have any friends we could introduce to him?"

She shakes her head. "It's too late for that unless Joann sends him away, and I doubt she'll do that. She needs financial help until she gets a few paychecks. I have her labeled as a user."

"Yes, and I'm afraid Doug Miller will never see that until she breaks his heart."

Tuesday afternoon, Joe Hawk calls. "Anna, I have a meeting in Fayetteville on Friday morning and would like to stop by and visit with the boys on Thursday afternoon if it's not inconvenient."

"They will love that. Come for dinner, if you enjoy pot-roast. That's what Mary wrote on the menu for Thursday night, and you're welcome to spend the night at our little house. We have two extra bedrooms. Bart doesn't have a class on Thursday night. He'll want you to stay."

"Thanks, I'll do that. I'm eager to see your home, the boys and taste that pot roast. I hate hotels and eating alone in restaurants."

Joann works late on Thursday and comes to get Curt a few minutes after Joe Hawk arrives. Mary invites her and Curt to stay and eat. Anna can see that Joann and Joe are attracted to each other. After dinner, they sit in the sunroom and play games with the boys. At eight, Carol and Maddi excuse themselves and go to their rooms. Mary and Professor Dugan sit in the den watching television.

At nine, Mary comes into the room. "Hank, Bill, Danny, you boys have school tomorrow. It's time for bed."

Joe Hawk stands. "I'm sorry, Mary. I was having such a good visit that I didn't notice the time. Goodnight boys. I'll stop by for a visit the next time I'm in town. Bart, I'll follow you and Anna to your cabin." He walks outside with Joann and stands talking until Bart and Anna drive around to the front."

He tells Bart and Anna that he invited Joann to a show at the Walton Art Center on Friday night and that she accepted.

"What about Curt?"

"We'll take him with us. He's a nice kid, and she's beautiful. For the first time in my life, I believe in love at first sight."

Anna lays awake thinking about Detective Miller. He could not be more attentive and kind to Curt if they were related, biologically. Anyone can see that he is in love with Joann, but Joann and Joe Hawk have that special spark that does not show when she looks at Doug Miller. If she only knew of a sweet woman that might interest him; she sits upright in bed. "Karen Phillips, she's the one."

Bart turns over. "What? Are you all right?"

"I'm fine. Sorry, I didn't mean to wake you." She eases back under the covers. "Karen Phillips is perfect for Detective Miller. She has a six-year-old boy, and they love fishing and camping."

Bart mumbles, "Who is Karen Phillips?"

"She's the woman that cuts my hair. She's pretty, although not a knockout like Joann. Go to sleep. I'll tell you about her tomorrow."

Before going to her early class on Friday, Anna calls her friend. "Karen, are you and your son busy tonight? If not, I want to invite you to dinner. You said you wanted to see our house. Bart and I have Hank, Danny and Bill for the night; I'm sure Mark will have fun playing games with them, and I'm cooking your favorite—Mexican food."

"I'd love to. What can I bring?"

"Your son and a pretty smile. I have most of the dinner ready to pop in the oven."

"That sounds wonderful. I get off work at five thirty, so it will be about six thirty before I can get there. Is that okay?"

"That's perfect. I want to take some pictures for my new scrapbook, so make yourself beautiful."

She laughs. "It will take more than an hour to do that, but I'll do my best."

Anna invites Detective Miller, to come at five for a cooking lesson and to help prepare the dinner.

When Doug Miller arrives, Bart takes the boys to the barn to hang a sack swing from the sturdy two-by-six brace going across the center of the barn. "Make yourself at home, Doug. I promised to help the boys hang a swing, but I'll be in before you and Anna get the food ready."

Anna pours two cups of coffee and asks him to sit at the table. "Doug, Bart and I consider you a special friend and we hate to see you hurt. We know that you like Joann, but she has someone else in her life. She didn't mean to hurt you. She had such need when we found her, that she had no choice but to accept our hospitality."

A pained look covers his face. "But, I thought . . . ."

"Right now, you must have a hole in the pit of your stomach that feels like a rock quarry, but try not to think about her. I have a friend coming for dinner that had a similar experience; only it was her husband. He ran off with a secretary from the office where he worked and left her to support their son. She works as a hairdresser and does an excellent job of taking care of the boy. Karen doesn't have extra money for toys and movies, but they go fishing, swimming and camping when the weather is right."

He does not say a word, just sits staring out the window, looking sad.

"Maybe, you and Karen can help each other. She's a great gal—a Christian that's trying to teach her boy about forgiveness and love."

"You don't have to play matchmaker. I can get a girl, but I've never found one that seemed so perfect. I thought Joann was the one for me."

"I know you did. I could see it in your eyes, but she didn't feel the same. You'll find that perfect person. Don't give up. You're a great guy and a wonderful catch for some lucky woman. My friend Karen is also a wonderful person; give her a chance. By the way, she doesn't know I invited anyone else, so don't be surprised if she has the same sentiment as you."

Anna jumps from her chair. "We need to start dinner."

Detective Miller prepares Mexican rice, refried beans, and cheese dip with Anna giving instructions. Anna has an enchilada casserole ready to put in the oven and chocolate cake in a covered dish.

Karen and Mark arrive at exactly six-thirty. She is beautiful. Soft blond curls spill over a blue sweater that accentuates her deep blue eyes; the jeans and sweater fit her size ten figure in a way that would make any man notice. She and Mark hold hands as they walk across the yard singing Old Joe Clark with animation. "Knock, knock, your entertainment is here." Karen and Mark laugh as they tap on the door.

Anna opens the door with Bart and Doug Miller behind her. "Come in. I heard your song. Did you bring your guitar?"

"Not mine, but Mark's getting good. Old Joe Clark is his latest song. I can't get it out of my head. I've been singing it day and night. Hello, Bart." She sticks out her hand to Doug. "I'm Karen, and this is my son, Mark."

"It's nice to meet you, Karen and Mark. I'm Doug Miller. So, Mark, you play the guitar?"

"I'm trying to learn, but I'm not very good. Mom's my teacher, and she's good; she plays several instruments."

Doug looks down, then back at her. "I try to play the guitar, but I'm a long way from good. Hank plays mandolin, and Bill is good on the harmonica. Bart plays the guitar and has a natural talent, but he never has time to practice. We might make some music after dinner."

While Anna and Karen put away the dishes, Hank, Bill, and Bart drag out their instruments. Doug brings in a fiddle and a guitar from his truck. "I don't usually tote these around, but I had new strings put on this afternoon."

Karen throws her drying towel on the cabinet. "You play the fiddle; that's my favorite, but mine got broken when we moved, and I haven't been able to afford another. My dad played Bluegrass and taught me when I was a little girl." She takes the fiddle from his hand and starts with Old Joe Clark. After the first few notes, she sings and pats her foot in time with the music. Mark sings loud and hearty; Bill bobs his head a few times to catch the beat and is playing along before Hank and Doug join.

"It's been over two years since I held a fiddle. Let me hear you play."

"Doug shakes his head. I can't play. I bought it to learn, but it sings in your hands. Hang on to it. I'll strum a little on my guitar. Enter in boys, we may have us a band. Anna, you or Danny need a set of drums."

Anna laughs. "I'll sing a little if the song's not too fast. I'm better at dancing. Karen, can you play 'Unchained Melody'. I know Bill can play it on his harmonica. That's Bart and my song; as kids, we learned to waltz to it."

The instruments almost speak the words. Bart holds out his hand to Anna. They melt together and waltz around the room. Hank sets aside his mandolin, and pushes back the table and chairs. Anna dances with all the boys, but Karen never turns loose of the fiddle. Doug Miller rarely takes his eyes off the blue-eyed blond. A spark gleams in both of their eyes and admiration shows on Mark's face.

Danny plugs in the coffee pot and cuts the chocolate cake while everyone else is playing music or dancing. When they stop to eat he asks, "Anna, do you think Aunt Mary and Uncle Charles will let me have a set of drums? They shouldn't make too much noise if I practice in the basement."

"I bet they would if you don't wait until bedtime to practice."

"Do you think a drum set is too expensive for me to request as a Christmas gift?"

"Maybe not. I'm not sure of the cost."

The boys are in bed, and the taillights of Karen and Doug's trucks have faded into the night when Joe Hawk steps onto the porch. Bart opens the door. "Come inside, Joe. We still have hot coffee, if you want a cup."

"I'd love one for the road. I'm driving home tonight. Coffee should help to keep me awake, although, I'm not the least bit sleepy."

"When do you think you'll come this way again?"

"Soon. I think I'm falling for Joann, and anyone would love Curt. He's quite a kid."

A frown wrinkles Bart's forehead. "Go slow, buddy. Make sure she feels the same and date for a while before making permanent plans."

He drinks the coffee, hugs Anna and shakes Bart's hand. "I love your home. It reminds me of the area where I grew up. Maybe someday, I'll have a home and family and can invite the two of you for a visit—or the five of you. I wouldn't want to neglect the boys."

"We'll look forward to that."

Later, Anna snuggles next to Bart on soft flannel sheets. "Now, Joe's caught in Joann's charms. I hope she's not leading him on to toss aside for the next handsome man that comes along."

"He's a good looking man and bound to have lots of pretty women after him."

"I'm sure of it, but Joanne is exceptionally beautiful. Not many compare with her."

Moonlight filters through window curtains. Coyotes howl in the distance, and logs in the wood stove shift and pop. "I wish I had a magic wand, and could wave away unhappiness and replace it with joy." She closes her eyes and whispers prayers.

Chapter Thirteen

Early Saturday morning Anna wakes to the scent of fresh coffee. Slipping into a robe and warm slippers, she goes to the kitchen. Bart and the boys are dressed and sitting at the table eating scrambled eggs and toast. "How did you keep from waking me?"

Bart grins. "We tried our best to disturb you. We dropped lids, banged pans together, and we've been talking loud, but you were awake most of the night trying to solve everyone's problems. You tossed, turned, and mumbled in your sleep. Have some coffee and eggs. We couldn't wait on you. The cement truck should arrive by eight."

"Oh, Bart. I wish I had set my alarm."

"No need to worry. We're ready. Eat your breakfast. Just be ready to write the driver a check before he leaves."

Anna gulps a cup of coffee and eats a few scrambled eggs before getting dressed. When the truck arrives, she is ready with a cement hoe to help drag the mud into place. Before noon, the storage room floor is level except for a slight slope to drain water to the outside. Each boy prints his name and the date before the mixture dries.

Lunch is serve-yourself with a loaf of bread, cheese, a pack of sandwich meat and a bag of chips tossed on the table.

The boys can hardly wait until Sunday afternoon when the floor will be dry enough to walk on. Danny brings a new hammer from the bedroom. "Anna, did you see the hammers Uncle Charles bought for us? He even had our names burned into the handles. Bart said we'll use the nail guns more than these, but I'm proud of mine just the same."

"That's nice. Hang onto it. When you are an old man, you'll want to show it to your grandsons. Maybe you'll become a famous architect, planning and constructing fine buildings. Then you'll want to hang it on the wall behind a fancy desk with a glass top and tell people that it was your first hammer."

He grins. "I like the way you think."

Reaching to give him a hug, she says, "Danny, remember you can become anything you want to be if you're willing to work for it."

Sunday morning, Mary orders fried chicken for pickup after church. While the boys change into work clothes, she and Anna set it on the table with paper plates and drinks.

Doug, Karen, and Mark are waiting in the driveway when Bart and Anna arrive at the new barn with the boys. Doug brought two nail guns, and Bart has two. Bart has already given Hank and Danny extensive safety instructions on their use. Bill and Mark will not use them.

Bart gives directions on how he wants the building constructed. Anna and Karen make coffee and hot chocolate for the workers, and they build a small fire in front of the barn to burn scrap wood. They huddle near the fire and keep a close watch on Bill and Mark. At least they think they are watching them closely.

While Anna and Karen talk, the little boys drag dead wood and toss it onto the fire. Instantly, the branches of a cedar tree ignite and shoot flames higher than the barn roof. The men and older boys run outside yelling. Bart hooks a hoe onto a lower limb and pulls the tree away from the barn.

Bart does not say anything, but Hank yells, "What were you guys thinking? You could have burnt the barn. Bill, you know better. Don't you remember Grandpa telling us to be careful with burning pine and cedar trees? They have turpentine in them—it flames and burns fast."

Bill drops his chin to his chest and looks as if he might cry.

Mark's eyes are wide with fear as he watches the tree crackle and burn. He tugs on Bart's coat sleeve, "It's my fault. I put that bush in the fire. I didn't know it would flame so fast. Bill was on the other side of the yard. He didn't do it."

"Thanks for telling us, Mark. Part of being a man is facing your mistakes and not letting someone else take the blame. Next time you'll know better than to push a cedar tree into a camp fire."

Hank puts an arm around Bill. "I'm sorry. I should have asked before yelling at you."

Bart turns to the boys. "If you want to burn brush, we'll do that after the next snow. I'm going to set those ditches on fire where we piled limbs cut from the cedar barn poles. I'll have to alert the volunteer fire department. That many limbs will make quite a fire. We have three ditches full of them."

"Bart," Danny calls, "Can we roast wieners over the coals?"

"I don't think so. They would taste like turpentine. "We'll build a fire with dry oak when you want to cook outside."

The storage room walls go up quickly, followed by sturdy shelves and hooks for hanging ropes and garden tools. Hank and Bill are eager to move everything from Grandpa's barn to the storage room. "Bart and Anna, you can use our tools anytime you want, we just don't want Uncle Al taking them to a pawn shop."

"Anna, next week will you take me around to the resale and antique shops? I heard Aunt Mary say she would like to have some old-fashioned glass covered bowls. I noticed some when I went shopping with Grandma."

"We can go for an hour after school on Monday before I have to rush home and start dinner."

"That's good. If I don't find any, maybe we can look another day."

"Sure, we'll check every shop in town until we find them."

The first shop they enter is close to home. "Hank, I bet they have dishes here, but they will be expensive. We can always return after shopping around a bit."

He nods and enters the store. On a quilt rack, near the window is a beautiful quilt. It has a squash blossom pattern with vibrant colors. "Where did you get that quilt?" Hank asks the sales clerk.

"A young Cherokee woman brought it in. The work is intricate and beautiful. Most young people don't have the patience to complete a quilt like that. I've been asking a thousand for it, but if you pay cash, I'll sell it for nine hundred."

"Anna, call Detective Miller. That is my quilt. Grandma made it for me. I bet Joann took it."

While they wait for the detective, the storekeeper tries to give the quilt to Hank. "The woman appeared so desperate for money that I didn't doubt her word. Take the quilt and go. I don't want any trouble. I wouldn't have bought it if I'd thought it was stolen."

"How much did you pay for it?"

"She asked two-hundred."

"But how much did you give her?"

"One-hundred. She seemed pleased with that."

"How much for the other one?"

"What do you mean? What other one?"

Anna has never seen Hank so angry. His dark eyes squint, and he keeps clenching his fists.

"You know what I mean. Did you give her the same for the red one?"

Her face is rosy, with beads of moisture on her forehead—reluctantly she answers, "Yes. The same for it."

"Where is it? It belongs to my brother."

"I sold it to someone passing through. I have no idea where it is?"

"You better find out. My grandma made those quilts, and she died a few weeks ago. They are priceless to me. Buying and selling stolen property is against the law."

When Detective Miller arrives, the woman produces a check taken in payment for the red quilt. The detective calls and gets a phone number and address of relatives where they are staying. After he tells them about the stolen quilt, they promise to return it to the police department.

Hank and Anna stop at a hardware store and buy new door locks. Hank, Danny, and Professor Dugan replace the old ones. When Joann returns after work, Hank has her belongings packed in trash bags and waiting on the carport. Detective Miller takes her and her son to the police station.

"Anna, I tried to help her. We all did, but she stole from us. How could someone steal from a friend?"

"This world has all kinds of people. Maybe she learned to

steal from her dad's example."

"We need to check the house carefully. Grandma packed those quilts inside boxes at the top of her closet. Joann probably sold Grandma's dishes too. We had lots of antique dishes—including a set of bowls like Aunt Mary wants, but I want to keep Granny's dishes. Where can I store them?"

"Maybe Bart will help you build cabinets in the Dugans' basement, but I think we better check and make sure Joann hasn't sold them, too."

"I've never hit a girl or woman, but if she sold Grandma's pink dishes, I might bust her nose."

"That wouldn't do a bit of good."

"It might make her think twice before she steals again."

"No, it won't. It will just get you put in jail. Joe Hawk might help her next time instead of you."

"Do you think he'd help a thief?"

"I don't know. She's beautiful, and he was crazy about her."

"I feel sorry for little Curt, but not her."

Except for a large platter, The antique, pink dishes are still at the house, packed in boxes, ready for hauling away. "Anna, she was planning to sell them too."

Anna calls the detective and describes the platter. Joann confesses to selling it to a jewelry store downtown. The store still has it, but a customer has paid a deposit toward the purchase.

Anna calls Joe Hawk and explains what Joann has done and that she is at the police station. She also tells him about how Joann led Detective Miller to believe she cared for him, let him spend money on her and then dumped him.

"Thanks for telling me, Anna. I was falling for her. She is

beautiful and seemed sweet, but being a lawyer has made me skeptical. I ran a background check—discovering that she has cheated more than one man, and she is wanted for theft in a northern state."

"Oh, no. I hate to hear that. Poor little Curt will be the one to hurt most. Hank was afraid you would come to defend her. He's determined to press charges, even though she's his cousin."

"I won't defend her, but I'll stand by Hank if he needs me, and tell Detective Miller that I wouldn't have taken her out if I'd known about him."

"Hank will be glad to know that you won't contend against him if the case goes to court. Detective Miller has met a wonderful girl and is glad that Joann is no longer a part of his life; another officer took her case."

Hank and Bill store the valuables from their grandparents' house in the Dugans' basement. Danny did the same with his. Maddi did not find anything in her Granny's apartment that she wanted to save.

Chapter Fourteen

Detective Miller stops by for a visit and tells Anna and Mary that a judge ordered Joann extradited to the northern state where she and a boyfriend will face theft charges. Curt will remain is DHS custody. "I don't have much sympathy for her, but my heart aches for that little boy. He cried and begged the officer not to take his mother. After they took her away, he asked the woman from DHS to take him back to stay with his cousins, Hank and Bill, at his Aunt Mary's."

Mary looks surprised. "I forgot about him calling me Aunt Mary. He thinks since Hank and Bill are his cousins, that I'm his Aunt because they live with us."

Anna turns toward the window. "Curt needs a stable family to guide his rebellious personality; whoever takes him may get a handful. Although, at first, I thought that about Maddi and she turned out great."

Mary lifts a Thanksgiving card that Maddi made for her. "Maddi was starved for love. Joann loved Curt but didn't give him proper guidance. Anna, I'm afraid you are right in thinking Curt might rebel. The other children get along well—I'd hate to disrupt our home with an uncooperative child."

Anna asks, "Doug, what did you think of Curt?"

"He's crazy about his mama, and he adores Bill, but he may have resentment against Hank for having Joann arrested."

Anna nods, "Yet, he might be good for Bill. Danny and Hank

are big buddies, Carol and Maddi stick together on everything, but Bill seemed like a tag-along until Curt came."

Mary shakes her head. "What am I thinking? Anna, we have enough responsibility. I have work, and you have school. Another child, especially if he's rebellious, might throw everything into chaos."

Anna stands. "Doug, do you want more coffee?"

"No, thanks." He looks at his watch. "I'm taking Karen to lunch. I need to go soon. How is your ankle?"

"It still hurts, but the doctor said I don't have to use crutches—only a cane."

After talking to Detective Miller, Hank drops the theft charges against Joann. That evening a social worker from DHS comes to talk to the Dugans about Curt. Anna excuses herself and goes to study until Bart comes for her.

The following morning Mary greets Anna at the door when she comes to take the children to school. "Anna, Charles and I agreed to take Curt on a trial basis. If he gives you any problems, let me know. Bill is happy that Curt's coming back. The other children didn't object or have any obvious response. I'll talk with Curt and tell him that he has to obey you just as he will Charles and me. I also want him to know that because Hank is the oldest child, and very responsible, he should abide by Hank's advice and instructions. Hank and Danny have individual bedrooms in the basement, but Bill said he is glad to have Curt share a room with him."

"I hope it works out well. I know he's a lonely little boy without his mother. I'll do my best to help him."

"Thank you. I offered Hank extra allowance to help with him, but he refused, saying he didn't want pay for helping with a little brother. Danny and Bill are self-reliant, but Curt is only four and needs more guidance."

"Mary, will you still take Curt to daycare?"

"Yes, and I'll pick him up in the afternoon, so the other children can start on homework when they get home."

Everything works fine, except the Sunday school teacher says Curt will not participate in class. Anna starts reading Bible stories to the four younger children while Hank and Danny do homework. Maddi and Bill ask countless questions. Carol has heard the stories before. Curt pretends not to hear, but one day he asks, "Anna, do you believe that angels can fly and that they watch over us?"

"Yes. The Bible tells us that they do."

"How do you know that's true? Some of the stories tell about a devil and Hell, but Mama said that there are no such things."

"Curt, maybe your mama didn't believe because no one taught her the things in God's word. The Bible is God's word—it tells us of his laws and his love. It also tells us about bad things caused by the Devil. Until the Devil tempted Eve, everything was good. When she disobeyed God, sin came into the world—that is when death started. Until then no one died."

"So, do you think Mama is gonna die because she did a bad thing?"

"No. Everyone's old flesh body will die someday. But if we believe in Jesus, confess and ask forgiveness for our sins, are baptized and remain faithful we'll go to heaven and live forever in a spirit body—no flesh and bones—just spirit."

He grins. "Do you mean that we can fly around in heaven, like Casper?"

She rubs his back. "Maybe; I only know we'll have spiritual bodies."

He stares at her and does not say more.

Maddi jumps up and waltzes around the room. "We'll float around heaven—happy ever after."

Carol squirms in her chair. "Anna can we go ride the horses?"

Anna glances at the clock. "Each of you can ride once around the yard, and then you have to come inside. It'll be dark soon, and dinner is almost ready."

Mary comes down the stairs after the children go outside. Anna tells her what Curt said. "I'm not sure I gave him an answer that he could understand. Do you want to explain it to him?"

"Let's let him think about it for a while. I'll ask the preacher if he can give us a better answer that a four-year-old can understand."

At dinner, Mary asks the children to make Christmas lists. "Put one thing that you want most of all at the top of your list. You may not get it, if it is not appropriate for your age or if it is too expensive, so you need to list some alternates."

Carol and Maddi rush to the sunroom, to work on their lists. Giggling as they go, Carol says, "Let's wish for bikes."

Maddi stops. "No. I want a horse."

"I don't think you'll get that. Mama complains all the time about two horses in our backyard. Maybe you should ask next year after Daddy gets a pasture fenced, so they're not in the yard all the time."

"Do you think they'll let us ride bikes outside the yard?"

"Probably not, unless everyone has bikes, and we all ride together."

Maddi giggles. "Then we better wish bikes for everyone."

Curt and Bill come to the table with paper and pencils.

Carol asks, "Curt, why do you look so sad?"

"I don't know what to ask for, and I don't know how to write. How can I make a list?"

"Decide what you want and I'll write a list for you. Maddi and I are asking for bikes."

"I don't know how to ride a bike."

Bill puts an arm around Curt's shoulders. "I have an old bike in Grandpa's barn. Tomorrow, we'll pump up the tires, and I'll teach you how to ride."

Danny is the first to give Mary his list. "I only want one thing. If a set of drums is too expensive, will you save the money so I can add to it until I get enough? I'll practice in the basement, and I won't wait until bedtime."

"How much do they cost?" she asks.

"I don't know. I don't even know what I'll need, but I want to learn how to play drums."

Mary smiles and pats his shoulder. "We'll check into it. Don't you have a birthday coming up the same week as Hank's?"

He nods with a grin. "It'll be fine if you combine my birthday and Christmas gift."

Hank asks for two new tires for his grandpa's truck and a driver's license permit.

Bill asks for new tires for his old bike.

Carol wants a bike.

Maddi hands Mary a folded paper. "I want a dog like Curly, something all my own to love, and something that will love me more than anyone else."

"Curly belongs to us all."

Maddi looks puzzled. "Carol said Curly was her dog, but he sleeps under Danny's bed and follows him around, so I know he loves Danny best. I want a dog that will love me best."

Curt takes his paper to Mary. "I can't write, and I don't know what to ask for; an old bike like Bill's will be okay. He's going to teach me to ride."

Hank's fifteenth birthday is December tenth. Professor Dugan brings home a Drivers Manual for Hank. "Son, study this for a few days, and then I'll drive you to take your test for a learner's permit."

Hank is ready by Friday and passes the test without a problem. Professor Dugan goes with him to get the truck, and they drive to a tire store where the professor orders four new tires mounted, aligned and balanced. "If my boy's going to drive, I want him to drive on safe tires." Before going home, they stop at a music store, buy a drum set and six months of lessons for Danny. "Music is part of education. If Danny is willing to learn, I want to help him."

The next day Hank brings his truck to the old garage behind the Dugan house. Danny helps him wash, wax and buff it until it shines. Professor Dugan gives him permission to leave his truck in the garage. "Bart has a parking place at his new home."

Carol and Maddi sit on the front steps watching Bill teach Curt to ride a bike. Every fifteen minutes, they have to pump more air into the old tires. Curt rides down the hill, turns into a driveway and peddles back without falling. Bill and the girls cheer as if he has won a state championship.

Bill straightens his shoulders and asks, "Do you girls want to learn?"

Carol jumps up. "We have to learn. We put bikes on our Christmas list."

"Okay, but don't cry when you fall. Everybody falls a few times when learning."

Maddi squints. "I won't cry. I'll go first."

Before dark, both girls have skinned elbows, hands, and knees, with the knees and elbows torn from their shirts and jeans, but they can ride down the hill—sometimes back. Neither girl has shed a visible tear.

Carol plops onto the lawn beside Maddi while Curt takes another turn. "If I'd known that it would take this much work and pain to ride a bike, I might have asked for more Barbie dolls."

Maddi pats a bleeding knee with a tissue. "I didn't ask for a bike. I asked for a dog like Curly."

"You did! I don't want to ride by myself. I guess we'll have to learn to ride double."

They slap hands and grin. "Well, if you share your bike, I'll share my dog, but it has to sleep under *my* bed."

On Christmas Eve, snow is falling. Carolers from different church groups stroll along the street, stopping when offered cookies and hot drinks. Mary asks Hank and Danny to set a table near the sidewalk with a platter of cookies and a three-gallon thermos of spiced, apple cider. Carol and Maddi take turns with Bill and Curt at pouring sweet cider and passing out cookies.

It is almost dark when Doug Miller, Karen, and Mark park on the street. They stand outside and sing with a group of carolers until the crowd moves on. Mary and Anna are placing vegetables and a huge ham on the dining table when they come inside, still singing.

Karen sets three pie-carriers on the counter. "I brought a chocolate and two pecan pies."

After dinner, Bart lifts Curt to place the Christmas Angel on top of the tree while Professor Dugan reads the Christmas story. Mark snuggles next to Karen. Hank and Danny sit on the floor leaning against the wall. Bill leans against Bart and receives a hug. Curt crawls onto Anna's lap pulling her arms around him. Carol and Maddi cuddle under Mary's arms.

At the end of the story, Professor Dugan says a prayer of thanks for family and good friends. Doug Miller, Karen, and Mark leave. The children say goodnight.

Anna whispers to Mary, "I'll let myself in with my key if you're not up when I get here in the morning. I want to have the casserole and rolls baking before the kids wake."

Mary reaches to hug her. "I'll set my alarm. See you in the morning."

Anna and Bart leave for their home.

Bart slaps at the alarm; it seems as if they have only been in bed a few minutes. "I think I'd rather have sleep than breakfast."

Anna groans and turns on a lamp. "Stay in bed—you can use an extra hour. I'll phone you when Mary gets up. I have to put a casserole in the oven."

He wraps the quilt tighter. "Are you sure you don't mind?"

"Consider it a Christmas gift. You miss a lot of sleep because of school." She slips from the bed and runs to the bathroom.

The Dugan house is quiet and dark when Anna arrives, except for a dim nightlight in Carol's room. Anna unlocks the door and tiptoes to the kitchen. Only turning on the stove light, she takes the casserole from the fridge and slides it into the cold oven and then sets the temperature.

A large pan with the ingredients for chocolate gravy, except milk, sits on the stove. She takes the thawed yeast rolls from the refrigerator, places them on the counter to warm and rise a little more. Adding milk to the chocolate mix, she begins to stir. Still, no sounds resonate in the rest of the house.

Leaning on the counter, she stirs, jumping when Maddi slides an arm around her. "Merry Christmas, Anna. Thank you for being so good to me. I love you."

Clicking off the burner and letting the large spoon rest against the side of the pan, Anna squeezes Maddi in a tight hug. "I love you, too."

"Is that chocolate I smell?"

"It's chocolate gravy to pour over buttered rolls."

"Wow. This is my first real Christmas breakfast. Mama always got drunk on Christmas Eve, and I had to be quiet all day or get in trouble. Last year, I tiptoed out of the house and went to a church that served lunch. They let me help and gave me cookies for washing tables. They gave me the first plate, let me eat in the kitchen, and said I was the official taster."

Anna dips chocolate into a small bowl and hands it to Maddi. "Will you be my official taster?"

Maddi giggles. "I was hoping you'd ask." She takes a spoonful and blows to cool it. Licking her lips after the first bite, she dips another. "This is about the best thing I ever tasted."

Anna bends to kiss the top of her head. "I'm glad you like it. I'll give you a little more but not much. Mary might get angry if I spoil your breakfast."

"Nothing spoils my breakfast. I'm always hungry."

"Is anyone else awake?"

"No. I thought Carol was going to talk all night. She was

excited about the presents she'll get." She sits motionless for several seconds with a solemn look.

"I don't think I'm getting a dog. It would be making noise, and I don't hear a thing."

"You may have to wait until summer, so you'll be near all day to train it. It's sometimes hard to housebreak a dog when no one is around to take it outside."

"Yeah, I didn't think about that."

Carol yells from upstairs. "Maddi. Maddi, where are you?"

Maddi slides off her chair and runs.

Bart knocks on the back door; Hank, Danny, Bill, and Curt come rushing in behind him. Hank stares into the pot of chocolate, sniffing as steam rises. "Bill and Curt woke an hour ago, so we've all had showers. Now, we're starved; chocolate never smelled this good. Are we going to eat first?"

Anna takes four rolls from a pan, hot out of the oven, tears them in half, drops them in soup bowls and dips a large spoon of chocolate over each. "Take this to the sunroom, eat quickly, and then put your bowls in the dishwasher." She gets no argument.

They have the bowls rinsed and in the dishwasher before the house hums with conversation. The boys sit whispering until Mary invites everyone to the Christmas tree. Six bikes, with a child's name taped to each, sit around the tree. Hank and Danny have heavy-duty mountain bikes.

Carol yells, "I'm starved, and I smell the chocolate gravy. Let's eat so that we can ride bikes."

The children wolf down breakfast and roll their bikes onto the sidewalk. Mary pushes a roasting pan, with a prime rib roast, into the oven. Bart and Professor Dugan go outside to watch the kids ride. Mary bundles in a warm coat to follow them. "Anna, we can eat dinner later in the day. Come watch the kids ride."

"You go on. I'll put vegetables on to cook and let the air outside warm a little before I go. My ankle still aches when it gets cold."

Maddi comes running in to get a drink as Anna takes two pies from the oven. "I fell twice, but I didn't hurt myself."

Before she goes outside, Anna asks, "Are you terribly disappointed that you didn't get a dog?"

"I'm not disappointed about anything. This is the best Christmas a kid could have. It's my first *real* Christmas." She throws a kiss to Anna before closing the door.

Bart comes in to get a tissue, his nose dripping from the cold air. "Do you need help? I want to stay inside and get warm."

Anna kisses his cold cheek. "Take the roast from the oven. That'll warm you."

Chapter Fifteen

After dinner, Hank and Danny go into the fields behind the house to ride their mountain bikes. Mary and Anna are cleaning the kitchen when Hank and Danny come rushing inside, both talking at once. "Call Detective Miller—we found a dead woman."

Anna scrolls to his name on her cell phone and pushes the button. He and other officers arrive and ask the boys to lead them to the location. Mary stays to read to the younger children, but Professor Dugan goes with the boys. Bart and Anna follow in his truck.

In a ravine, where the boys piled cedar branches, lies a young woman. She is fully dressed, but not wearing a coat or gloves. Her hands and face show severe bruising.

The professor says, "She looks familiar. She may have been a student at the college." Officers question him, but he cannot remember where he has seen her.

"Professor, search your memory and give us a call if you remember anything that can help identify her. We haven't found a purse or wallet."

Danny tells the officers that a red, older model, Ford truck pulled out of the field and took off down the road, spinning tires as they approached on their bikes. Hank adds, "We could only see one person in the truck and the license plate was too dirty to read the numbers."

Prior to reporters arriving, Anna walks close looking at the woman. Even with dark bruises on her face, Anna can tell that she was extremely attractive. Staring at the golden blond hair, Anna shivers and remembers the mention of a beautiful woman with gold hair.

Anna leans on Bart, her legs trembling. "We need to go home. I'm tired, but will you ask Detective Miller to stop by our house before he returns to the station."

"Why? If you're tired, you need to take a nap. We got to bed late last night, and you were up early."

She frowns. "Just ask him, please. I'll explain in the truck."

"Okay." He walks away.

Anna makes a pot of coffee and sits in the rocker waiting for it to stop gurgling. She pours herself and Bart mugs of the strong black liquid and takes two more cups from the shelf when she sees Detective Miller and Professor Dugan pull into the driveway.

They take coffee and sit at the table. "Anna, what did you see that you felt we need to discuss?"

She wraps her hands around the hot mug and stares into it. "I feel a little silly for asking you to come by, but I remembered Maddi saying her mama was beautiful with gold hair. I know there are lots of beautiful blonds in this town, but could that woman have been in this area looking for Maddi?"

Professor Dugan snaps his fingers. "I know where I saw her. She was on our street the afternoon Bill was teaching the girls to ride a bike. She parked some distance from where the kids were riding. I noticed her standing beside a red truck and thought she was holding binoculars. I went to Carol's room, got those old field glasses I gave her to play with and looked out the window. I'm sure that is the same woman, and she was driving an old, red, Ford truck. A bush in the neighbor's yard hid my view of the plates. It was getting late, so I called the children inside. I forgot all about that until now."

Anna twists the mug in her hands. "That's an affluent neighborhood; people pay attention when an old vehicle stops on the street. Maybe one of the neighbors got a plate number."

Doug Miller nods. "We'll check with everyone living nearby. I know the children received new bikes for Christmas, but I suggest keeping the kids in your backyard until we know more about this situation. Kidnapping could have been a motive that went awry."

Across from where Professor Dugan saw the woman and the red truck parked, a woman active in the Neighborhood Watch Program, took a picture—it clearly shows the young blond and the license plate.

Doug Miller stops to talk to Bart and Anna. "Investigators had no trouble finding the truck's registered owner. He swears it was stolen and claims he did not report it because he thought his girlfriend took it. She is missing too. He figured she was irate again and decided to let her stew a while."

"Do you think the boys might identify him as the driver?

"They said they didn't get a good look at him, but we'll do a lineup. Maybe they'll remember something."

"When we questioned him further, he said, 'Twila has a kid, a hateful little brat. I planned a trip to Vegas and told Twila she could go, but no way was I taking that kid. She promised to leave the girl with her mother. We talked marriage, but she decided she wanted to come back for the kid. I told her it was me or that brat.'"

"Doug, do you think it might be Maddi?"

"It is. Now, we've got to find that grandma."

"I need to talk to Mary and Professor Dugan. They should make sure Maddi doesn't see the pictures on TV."

The children are sad when told they are not to ride their new bikes. They mumble but do not question the decision. The weather is cold and drizzling rain for the remaining days of Christmas break. Mary tells Maddi about her mother's death and that Detective Miller thinks it is dangerous for her to attend the funeral.

"I don't want to go. She was alive when she left me. I want to keep you as my mama."

"All right, Maddi. That's how it will be, as long as the courts will let you stay with us."

* * * * *

School resumes the first full week in January. The boys return, but Maddi and Carol have colds. Mary tells them they must stay home—she and Anna will tutor them. Mary goes to work an hour later. Anna rushes back to the Dugan home after her last class.

Anna hears Charles whisper to Mary, "You can't continue to keep those girls at home without registering them in a home school program."

Frowning, Mary keeps her voice low. "I know, Charles. The police have not discovered anything new, except to confirm that woman was Maddi's mother. I'm afraid to let the girls outside until we know who killed her and why."

"We may never know that."

"Maybe not, but I keep praying for an answer."

He puts his arms around her and pulls her close. "Mary, I'm praying too, but we have to make a decision. Carol and Maddi are too smart to spend another year in kindergarten. If their birthdays were a few days earlier, they could have gone to first grade this year, and they would have done well."

"Oh, Charles, I know they need to be in class. I'll meet with the teacher tomorrow, explain the situation, ask her not to let the children wait outside the classroom after school, and I'll take them on Tuesday."

Monday afternoon, Mary calls. "Anna, I received a call from DHS. Maddi's grandma has decided she wants custody of Maddi. My lawyer says that unless a judge decides living with the grandma will be bad for Maddi, we will probably lose her. A hearing is set for next week. I don't know how they arranged it so quickly, but we will stand up for Maddi. Our lawyer is coming tonight to visit with her."

"Do you want dinner at the usual time?"

"Yes, and I'd like you to explain this to Maddi and ask her where she wants to live. Ask her how she was treated when she stayed with her grandma. Also, tell her that she will have to talk to a judge and explain it all to him or her."

Anna calls the girls downstairs, gives them a fruit snack, and relays Mary's message.

Immediately, tears form in their eyes. "No, please don't let her take me," Maddi begs. "She's mean. She only wants the money those people give to pay my expense. That's the reason she didn't want me before. Mama said she had to have that money and the food stamps. They didn't want me; they only wanted that check and argued about it all the time."

"Did you get good meals while at your grandma's?"

"Never. If I walked to school in time to get it, I got free breakfast after I started kindergarten. I got free school lunch, but grandma never cooked supper. She said lunch was enough for me. On weekends, I walked to the park or the library if it was raining. Granny always had a headache from drinking wine and got mad if I woke her."

Anna glances at the spindly child, noticing that she has gained weight since she came to live at the Dugan home. "What about breakfast?"

"Sometimes, after the breakfast or lunch crowd left the restaurant on the corner, I'd go inside and help Miss Smith wash tables and put dirty plates on a cart. At first, I'd sneak leftover food off the plates. After she noticed and told me not to do that anymore, she sat me in a corner and always brought me a plate of something good to eat. She was nice."

"How old were you?"

"Same as now; it was just a while before I came here. When I was little, I was always hungry."

"You have to tell the judge everything. Tell the exact truth, and tell him where you want to live."

Anna wants to sit and cry with the girls, but that would serve no purpose. "Maddi, did your mama tell you anything about your dad?"

"She said he was not handsome, but he's rich and smart, and that I look like him. See this red mark under my chin—he has one on his right hip, and I have his dark hair and blue eyes. She was going to try to make him give her money for me, but she never did. Granny told her he would take me away, and she'd lose the food stamps and rent money."

Anna refastens a barrette over Maddi's ear. "Was your

mama good to you?"

"Better than Granny. I was not as hungry when Mama was home. She gave me a little purse, and I found a picture of my daddy inside. It's just a newspaper picture, and it's not very good, but I kept it."

"What did you do with the purse?"

"I still have it. It's not big. I used to keep it in my jeans pocket all the time—now I keep it in my room."

"Hon, I think you should show it to Detective Miller."

"Do you think my daddy killed Mama?"

"I didn't say that, but I think the detectives will want to ask him some questions. Maybe he knows someone else that wanted her killed."

"I want to see him, but I don't want him trying to take me away." Maddi stares at the window and folds and refolds her napkin. "I'm not sad that mama's dead—I'm not glad either. She didn't love me, not like you and Aunt Mary love Carol. I know it's a sin to wish somebody dead, but if it weren't, I might wish that for Granny. If I had lots of money, I'd give it to her to make her leave me alone. I like it here."

After the girls go to play, Anna calls Mary at work. "Mary, have you thought about trying to adopt Maddi? That grandma is not going to adopt her, and DHS will want her to go to someone that will pay all her bills."

"Yes. Charles and I plan to talk to our lawyer about adoption, but how do you think Danny, Hank, and Bill will react to that? We can't adopt them all. Those boys get pension money that we save for their education. We can't afford to send five children to college without help."

"Do you want me to talk to the boys about it?"

"If you get a chance, please do."

Hank and Danny rush to the kitchen after school, cold and hungry. Anna meets them at the door. "Wash your hands while I get snacks. I need to talk to you about something."

Hank is the first to sit. "Anna, what's wrong?"

She explains the situation concerning Maddi. "They love all of you, but you boys receive money from government pensions. Mary and Professor Dugan put that into a savings account for your college. You might lose that if they adopt you. Maddi doesn't get anything like that, only a little from DHS—which her selfish grandma wants to take. If they don't adopt Maddi, her Granny will take her away where she will not get enough to eat. Remember how pathetic she looked when she first came here?"

They all nod and Danny asks, "Well, why don't they adopt her?"

"They are worried that you boys will be upset."

Hank shakes his head. "We're a family. A family does what needs to be done to help each other—right Danny?" They nod and slap hands. "Anna, will you call Aunt Mary and tell her that we understand. We don't want to lose little Maddi."

Mary tells Anna that she and Professor Dugan have already instructed their lawyer to file adoption papers. The children shout and hug each other when they hear the news.

While Carol and Anna put away dinner dishes, Maddi sits in the den with Mary, Professor Dugan, and the lawyer. The lawyer tapes the conversation and tells them that he is sure the judge will not allow Granny to take her. Maddi's eyes overflow but she giggles, hugs Mary, and gives Professor Dugan a high five.

Detective Miller arrives in time for apple pie and coffee. Maddi shows him the picture and watches as he carefully goes through the small purse. "Maddi, will you allow me to borrow your purse and picture? I'll bring it back. I would also like to have a couple of hairs from your pretty head to put in my file."

"Sure. You can borrow the purse." She turns her head to the side and yanks two long hairs. "Here you go." Slinging hair over her shoulder, she grins. "Anna read us the story of Rumpelstiltskin. You're out of luck if you think you can spin my black hair into gold."

He chuckles. "Rumpelstiltskin is not my name."

Anna hands him a sandwich size zippered bag. "You can keep your knitting in this."

The next day Detective Miller brings the purse back. "Maddi, I took pictures of your purse. Inside the lining, I found a small flat key to a safety deposit box. The key is in our evidence locker. You'll get it later. We think whoever killed your mama may be searching for that key."

Her eyes widen. "Keep it. I don't want them after me."

"What did your mama say to you when she gave you the purse?"

Maddi closes her eyes and sits for a moment. "She said, 'Keep this, it may be the only worthwhile thing I can ever give you.'"

"Did it have anything else inside—money, papers, anything?"

She nods. "A paper with a number on it and a gold bow pin with a giant fake diamond in the center. I have the pin in the box with my Barbie doll. The paper may be in there too. I don't remember."

"Bring your doll box downstairs and let me take a look, please."

"Sure." She runs upstairs and returns with a large plastic box."

He turns the pin over in his hand several times, looks through the box until he finds a yellow scrap of paper with a number on it. "Maddi, I need to take these to the evidence locker. You'll get them back with your key."

A few days later, the phone is ringing when Anna enters the house after picking up the children. "Anna," Mary speaks quickly. "Will you tell Maddi to bathe and put on one of her best dresses? We have a preliminary hearing with a judge at five this afternoon. It might be a good idea for all the children and you to come with us. You and the other kids can wait outside unless the judge wants to speak with you. We'll go for pizza afterward. Maybe we'll still have time to go to Bible study after we eat."

At the courthouse, Anna, Carol, and the boys sit on a long bench in a hallway to wait while Mary, Professor Dugan, and Maddi continue down the hall. A slim man with dark hair and smoke blue eyes enters the hallway. Smiling directly at Anna, he states, "Good afternoon."

Anna says, "The same to you." From the bench, she wonders if he has a red birthmark on his right hip. A small oriental woman follows, almost running to keep up.

When the door closes behind the couple, Anna walks to the closed door, stands a moment, returns to sit, bite her lip, and twist her hands. Hank and Danny move to another bench and whisper. Carol sits in a corner reading a book about horses. Bill and Curt stretch onto the seat to color in Superman books.

Hank motions for Anna and mouths the words, "Sit with us."

She moves to sit next to him. Danny stands and leans close. "That guy looks like Maddi. I bet he's her dad. Do you think he'll try to take her?"

"I don't know. She's never met her dad."

Hank rubs his neck. "Poor Maddi. At least our grandparents loved us."

Chapter Sixteen

Minutes seem like hours until the Dugans come through the big double doors. Maddi clings to Mary then runs to hug Anna and Carol. "The judge said Granny can't take me. For now, I get to stay with you, but I have to visit with my dad."

The girls hug and slap hands. "My dad thought I was dead until Mama was killed, and Grandma wanted him to pay her money to tell where to find me."

Carol's eyes are wide and frightened. "Is he going to take you away?"

"He wants me to live with him and his wife, but for now I'll just visit every other weekend. Maybe you can go with me."

The man and his wife stand nearby holding hands and watching. "Maddi, your adopted sister and brothers can visit at our house anytime Mr. and Mrs. Dugan will allow."

Maddi and Carol grin and hug again. The boys, unsmiling, stare at him.

Professor Dugan whispers in Mary's ear—she nods. "Mr. Meeks, we promised to take the children for pizza. Would you and your wife like to join us?"

Smiles cover their faces. Mr. Meeks answers, "We love pizza. Thank you for the invitation, but why don't you come to our home? We'll order pizza delivered. That way Maddi and the children can become familiar with our home and we can visit without interruptions."

Professor Dugan looks at his watch and to Mary. "We'll be too late for Bible study after we eat." He turns to Maddi. "What do you think?"

Maddi shrugs. "Okay with me."

Mr. Meeks hands Professor Dugan a business card with his address on the back. "You can follow me if you wish."

Looking at the address, Professor Dugan grins. "I'm familiar with this street. You live a few houses down the block from our home."

"That is what the private detective, hired to find my little girl, said. I do not wish to cause her any unhappy moments. I'm sure she has already had more than her share of those. My wife, Ling, and I hope we can share happy times with Maddi, the children she calls her sister and brothers and with you as well."

They stop in the driveway beside a new two-story brick home. Perfectly manicured landscaping surrounds the house. Most of the shrubs are small, although one large oak tree stands as tall as the house. Winter has brushed away leaves, but Anna can tell that in summer the tree will be beautiful and cover the yard with cooling shade.

A housekeeper greets them in the entry and ushers them into a game room complete with a ping-pong and pool table. Large windows separate the room from an indoor swimming pool.

Mrs. Meeks speaks to the children, "You may play any of the games. Next time you visit, bring your swimsuits if you want to swim. We have games for entertainment but, unfortunately, we've missed sweet children to share them with."

The children, except Maddi, nod with excited expressions.

Danny says, "Sometimes in the summer, we go to Anna's farm and swim in the creek, but not since Maddi came to live with us. She'll go with us next year."

"I can't swim. I've never gone swimming." Maddi's voice is as solemn as her face.

Mr. Meeks pats her shoulder. "Ling is a good teacher. She used to teach at the YMCA." He directs his words at Maddi. "If the Dugans will allow, you and Carol can come over for lessons. We swim laps almost every evening before dinner."

"I need lessons too. I can't swim," Curt says.

Ling reaches a hand to him. Rather than take her hand, he snuggles against her wrapping her arm around his shoulders.

"What's your name young fellow?"

"Curt. I'm only staying for a few months. My mama went north to work, but soon she'll come back to get me."

"I'm sure she misses you very much and that you miss her."

"Yes, but she'll come back for me."

"I'm certain of that. Maybe when she comes back, you can show her how well you can swim." She turns to Mary. "It has been several years since I taught at the 'Y' but they should still have records, and here is a card from my present employment. Your children will be safe in our home, and you are welcome anytime you want to come with them."

"I'm confident of that, but I'll check your references as I believe any good parent would do in the interest of child safety."

Except for Curt, the children stuff themselves with pizza and play games. Curt hugs Ling and stays beside her all evening. Maddi participates but not joyfully. Her actions and expressions are serious.

At home, after the children go to their rooms, Anna sits to

talk with Mary while waiting for Bart to return from his last class. "Mary, did you notice how Curt clung to Ling, and how Mr. Meeks kept trying to touch and hug Maddi whenever she came close to him, but she kept her distance."

She nods. "I noticed. Ling, with her dark hair and eyes, favors Curt's mama, and he misses her badly. Ling didn't push him away. She may not have children of her own, but it seems she has some motherly instincts. We need to hug and show him as much love as we can. A four-year-old needs more special attention than the older ones."

Mary pauses before continuing. "I noticed a flash of anger in Ling's eyes when I told her I would check her references. Years of working in a counseling office has taught me to read facial expressions. I don't trust that woman."

"What about Mr. Meeks and Maddi?"

"He's a stranger to her. Charles and Bart are probably the first men she's been around that have shown her true kindness. She's happy here and may resent Mr. Meeks trying to interfere. On the other hand, he's missed years with his child and wants to hug and hold her close, but he'll have to be patient. Right now, she may classify him with the many men she has seen with her mama—some of them may have tried to touch her inappropriately."

"What a crazy world we live in." Anna stands. "Bart should be home in a few minutes." Turning toward the door, she stops and takes a deep breath. "Mary, I think I should send Hank along to help with Curt when the girls and Curt go for swimming lessons."

"That's a good idea. I'm sure he won't mind."

"He cares for them like a parent, but they respect him and

never seem to resent his warnings. If you don't mind, I want to check on Maddi before I go. I bet she's still awake."

Mary nods. "I wouldn't doubt it. This was an eventful day for her."

Anna tiptoes into Maddi's room and finds an empty bed. She rushes to Carol's bed. The two girls are side by side, with hands clasped together on top of the quilt. Carol is asleep, but Maddi's wide eyes stare at the ceiling. Kneeling, Anna whispers, "Do you need to talk?"

She works her hand free of Carol's, eases from the bed, and whispers, "Come to my room."

Anna turns back the covers. "Climb in, so you don't get chilled."

"I don't want to live with them. I want to stay here with Carol, the boys, you, Bart, Aunt Mary, and Uncle Charles."

Sitting on the side of the bed, Anna bends to kiss her forehead. "I could tell that, but they don't have other children. They want to love you and want you to love them in return. Maybe, that will eventually happen."

"I don't like him hugging me. Uncle Charles doesn't do that unless I reach for him."

"He reaches to hug Carol."

"Yeah, but he's always been her daddy."

"I noticed you trying to stay out of Mr. Meeks' reach. I understand. He's still a stranger to you."

"Some of Mama's old boyfriends tried to hug me. I want to be left alone."

"I think you handled it well. You avoided him without saying anything mean. If he does not get the hint, you may have to tell him that you know he is your daddy, but you don't want him to hug you—maybe someday but not now. If he insists, bluntly say to him 'I don't like hugging, if you want me to visit in your house, don't hug me.' Maddi, no one has a right to touch and hug you if you don't want them to."

"Not even my daddy?"

"That's right. Not even your daddy."

"Anna, sometimes I want to hug you and Aunt Mary, especially when I see you hugging Carol. A few times, even Uncle Charles, but at other times, I want to hit anyone that touches me. Once at the church an old man patted my hip. I gritted my teeth to keep from giving him a hard shove. Why do men think they can pat on girls? I think a woman should slap a man that touches her butt—why not girls, too?"

Anna breathes deeply. "It's not appropriate for a man to touch your bottom. My advice is to keep your distance from anyone that tries to touch you in any way that makes you feel uncomfortable. You lived in an environment quite different from Carol. She runs to her daddy for hugs. When he gives her a friendly slap on the bottom, she thinks nothing of it, but I suspect some of the men that your mother brought in tried to carry a pat into something inappropriate. Your daddy wants a daughter's affection, but to you he is a stranger, and I think you are wise for being cautious. Months from now, you may run to him as Carol does to Professor Dugan, but that should be your decision."

Maddi presses her lips to the top of Anna's hand. "Thanks for coming up. Now I can sleep."

Anna stands and pulls the quilt over Maddi's shoulders. "Anytime you want to talk; I'm here for you, little sister."

Anna hears Bart tap on the door and speak to Mary. "Will

you tell Anna that I'm going home? Two hard tests drained my brain. I need sleep. See you later, Mary."

Anna rushes to put on her coat and give Mary a quick hug before going to her car. The horses whinny from their stalls and the scent of their sweet hay wafts across the yard as she walks toward the old garage. She would like to throw a saddle on Polka and ride across the hills. It is a beautiful night for a ride—a bright moon illuminates everything—but Bart would worry if she is not home within a few minutes. She does not want to cause him stress.

Bart waits for her beside the barn and slides the heavy panel into place after she exits her car and steps outside. "Someday we'll get an automatic door, and you can push a button to open and close it."

She wraps her arms around him. "But it is so nice to have a handsome man standing nearby to open and close it."

He pulls her close. "I don't mind that at all, except when it's raining, snowing, or the cold wind is howling like banshees." He looks at the clear sky. "It's beautiful out tonight. I'd say let's go for a walk, but I'm worn-out, and I have another test tomorrow. How did the meeting with Maddi's granny go?"

"Thank goodness, Granny doesn't get her, but Maddi's dad and stepmom appeared. The Dugans have custody of her for now, but she will visit her dad every other weekend. Maddi is nervous about it, but they invited Carol to come with her any time, and the boys if they want. They have a beautiful house with an indoor pool. It's a few doors past the Dugan home."

"Wow. Figure a way to finagle us an invitation."

Grinning, she pokes him in the ribs. "Maybe, that will come with time. Maddi and Curt have never been swimming. The stepmom volunteered to give them lessons. Curt appeared to love her instantly, but Maddi keeps her distance."

"I hope this doesn't become too complicated."

"Maddi's thinking the same thing, but the other kids are excited—an indoor pool where they can swim year-round."

Bart unlocks the door. Stepping inside, he shudders. "Do you want me to build a fire? It's colder in here than outside."

"Not tonight. That would take at least an hour from our sleep time. The blankets will be warm. Let's get some sleep and talk more in the morning."

Bart is asleep within minutes. Anna goes over the events of the day—especially little Maddi's worries. It is rare, but she has heard of children molested by parents. She will ask the Dugans to insist that Mr. Meeks get a DNA test proving he is Maddi's biological father and ask Detective Miller to run a complete background check on him.

A few days later, Detective Miller calls, "Anna, are you away from the children where we can talk?"

"Yes, they're outside with the horses."

"We found the safety deposit box and opened it. Inside was a bag of jewelry reported stolen from the home of Mr. Meeks' mother. The pin Maddi had on her doll's dress was on the list of missing items. It's an antique worth more than the average person's home. That big diamond is real."

"How did Maddi's mama get them?"

"I wish we could ask her. The reported theft happened about six years ago. I figure Maddi's mama told a boyfriend about the jewels, he robbed the house, and she took them from him. That could be what got her killed."

"Do you think Maddi's granny knew about them?"

"That might be why she decided she wants Maddi. We plan to interrogate her, but we have to find her first. None of her neighbors admits to seeing her since last Wednesday."

Anna frowns. "She may wind up in a ditch like her daughter."

"I don't think Meeks is involved. His family is rich without the jewels. He has a doctorate, a well-paying job, and no criminal history; besides the jewels were insured."

"It's hard for me to comprehend the mentality of a mother and grandmother treating a child with such heartless ways as they did Maddi."

"I've seen it before. Abuse is usually passed on to following generations unless the children are taken away early and raised in better environments."

"I hope we rescued Maddi in time."

"I believe you did. She seems like a sweet kid."

"I think we should keep the news of the jewels secret until you solve the mystery."

"I hope we solve it soon. Reporters float around the station, bold as vultures."

Chapter Seventeen

Friday afternoon, Ling stops her sports car in the driveway, waiting for Maddi and Curt. Anna stands in the doorway, watching as Hank goes out with them and speaks to Ling. "Aunt Mary wants me to come along to help Curt while you teach Maddi."

Ling smiles. "I'm a teacher. I can handle more than one child at a time."

He straightens his back. "Aunt Mary asked me to come along. I won't get in your way."

"Do you mind walking? My little car only seats two passengers."

Curt, already in the car with his seatbelt fastened, smiles.

Maddi, with her new swimsuit slung over her shoulder, says, "I'll go with Hank." She walks away before Ling can answer.

Anna and Carol busy themselves with cooking dinner and watching the clock until Mary comes inside with Curt, Maddi, and Hank. "Anna, I stopped to get the children after you told me about her little sports car. I didn't want any of them walking in this wind with wet hair."

Maddi runs to her room. Anna hears her door slam. "Mary, is Maddi disturbed about something?"

"She and Hank didn't say a word on the way home, but Curt talked enough for them all. He's determined to learn and can already swim a few strokes. By summer, he'll be ready for the creek."

The next time Ling invites them to swim, Maddi says she has a sore throat and does not want to go.

Ling invites all the children to swim on the following Saturday. Hank and Danny promised Bart and Professor Dugan that they would help set fence posts for a new fence around the property, and Mary has shopping planned. Carol, Bill, and Curt are excited about going, but Maddi wants to stay home.

Anna closes Maddi's door and sits on the bed. "Okay, pretty little sister; tell me why you don't want to go."

"I don't like Ling. Can't I stay here or go with Bart, Hank, and Danny?"

"What did she do to make you so angry?"

"I thought she was gonna drown me. She kept telling me to straighten my body and paddle my feet, but I couldn't do it. My head was about to go down. She yelled, 'Straighten your legs and paddle your feet.' The next thing I knew she was holding my swimsuit and pushing on my back. I couldn't breathe or get away. I choked and started fighting."

Maddi looks away and takes a deep breath. "When Ling let go of me, I climbed out of the pool. She yelled for me to get back in, but Hank told her to let me alone. She said, 'I'm the teacher here, young man.' Hank said, 'I'm her brother, and I said, let her alone. She's upset and doesn't need to get back in the pool.' She returned to helping Curt, but Hank and I sat on a bench and watched until Aunt Mary came to get us."

"I'll go with you today, and I'll help you while she works with Curt; okay?"

Maddi nods and reaches to squeeze Anna's hand. "I think

she turned me loose because I hit her bruised arm."

"How did she bruise her arm?"

"I don't know. It was dark blue when she came to get us. The way she held it, I could tell it hurt. She had another bruise on the side of her face, but she'd tried to cover it with makeup."

Anna pulls sweat pants over her swimsuit before going to get her car. Maddi is relaxed and unafraid with Anna and is soon swimming better than Curt.

"Anna, do you think I'll be good enough by summertime, to swim in the creek?"

"I'm sure of it. Once you get over your fear of the water, you've got it made. With practice, you'll be a good swimmer."

Ling frowns and turns away to help Curt.

After an hour, Mr. Meeks comes to the pool. He and Bill play catch with a large rubber ball. While scrambling for the ball, Mr. Meeks jumps, and his swim trunks slide low on his hips. Anna does not see a red birthmark. Noticing Ling staring, she turns her head away.

That afternoon while the children take naps, Anna calls Detective Miller and relays what Maddi told her about the birthmark and Ling's bruised arm and face. He tells her he will try to get a copy of Mr. Meeks' birth certificate.

"Doug, if Meeks is an identical twin, will they have the same DNA?"

"Yes, that will be identical, but birthmarks can be different. We need to know where they had marks and scars like most kids receive during childhood. If he is an identical twin, we'll need to interview old nannies, teachers, and neighbors."

"I hope he doesn't discover that you are checking on him."

"I don't want to breathe a word about the possibilities until I know if Maddi's dad was a twin. I think someone knew about those jewels and wanted them bad enough to beat Maddi's mama because they thought she had them. They might not have intended to murder her."

"I'm afraid to let Maddi out of my sight. If Mary agrees, I think we should keep her at home next week."

"That's not a bad idea."

Anna talks to Mary about keeping all three of the kindergarten children home until the police know more about the murder.

"I hate to keep them home, but I do feel they will be much safer. Maybe, I can get one of the older women from church to stay with them."

Shaking her head, Anna says, "I would feel better if you or I stay with them. Everyone thought we had such a secure fort that Jaeger and his friends couldn't get to us, but they did. I want to be here with the kids as much as possible, with a loaded gun on my hip. I'm a good shot and not afraid to defend myself and my family."

"I'm sure they are safer with you than anyone else, but I don't want you to fall behind and lose your scholarship."

"I'll talk to my professors. I think they'll let me study at home as long as I come in for the tests."

Maddi and Carol stay home from church with Anna on Sunday. She reads them the story of Esther and spends over an hour answering questions and explaining. After lunch, Bart, Professor Dugan, and the boys go to work on the new fence. Mary declares that she has a briefcase full of work from her office.

Sitting in the sunroom, trying to read a textbook, Anna

wonders, "What happened to Maddi's granny?" She jumps when her cell phone rings. "Hello!"

"Anna, this is Miller. Meeks is an identical twin. We've already talked to a neighbor, a teacher, and we're trying to find a nanny that stayed with them when they were about eight. The neighbor is in his late eighties and lives in a nursing home, but he seemed confident in his memories. He said the boys were hard to tell apart, but one had a small white scar on his hand where a dog bit him. That one was always throwing rocks at neighborhood cats and dogs. Also, the dad began taking him hunting when he was very young, but he shot one of the guides, which started a big stir. The guide swore it was no accident and the dad paid him a handsome sum to drop the charges."

"He sounds like an evil child."

"The other boy was gentle, mannerly, and clearly his mother's favorite. The old man said one was a model child; the other was cruel and devious."

"What did the teacher report?"

"She's in a home, as well, and remembered the twins. She said they were both exceptionally brilliant, but different as night and day. One was kind and got along well with everyone. The other was spiteful, mean, and lazy. She often thought that the nice one did the homework for them both, so his brother wouldn't get in trouble. She suspected schizophrenia but came to the conclusion that Albert was lazy with an evil streak helped along by not receiving discipline from his parents."

"Did she give you any pointers on how to tell them apart?"

"She said the lazy one slanted his writing and put more curves into it. He had a white scar on his hand and one under his chin."

"I'll be sure to look for those when I see him again."

Hank and Danny rush inside. Danny speaks first. "We found another body. It was in another ravine where we piled brush, near the edge of your land. This one is a man. We saw buzzards circling and went to investigate."

Hank slumps into a chair. "I bet that guy in the red truck got scared when he saw us the other day and took off before he could dump the man's body. Lots of trees blocked our view of the second ravine."

"You may be right. Go wash your hands while I call Detective Miller."

Bill says. "I think Uncle Charles has already called him."

"I'll call, to make sure."

Detective Miller answers on the first ring. "Anna, I'm on my way. I'll get back to you when I know something."

She goes to help the girls prepare lunch. Carol is making lemonade, and Maddi is filling glasses with ice.

The last to come inside, Professor Dugan goes to wash his hands and face. "Carol will you make me a sandwich with pepper cheese on it?" With a sigh, he drops into a chair. "Mary, I can't keep pace with Bart and these boys. Just watching them makes me tired. All I do is drive the truck with the posts and cement and pull the water tank. Hank drills holes with his auger for the big corner posts and brace posts. Bill and Curt place rocks into the hole after Bart drops in a heavy railroad tie or a big cedar post. Danny tamps the stones with a wrecking bar before Bart pours dry concrete mix over the rocks and adds water. Between the corner and brace posts, Danny holds the regular steel posts straight while Bart or Hank drives them into the ground with a post driver. They have a system worked out that doesn't waste any time."

He clears his throat. "I tell you these boys are workers. It will take several days to build a fence around the property, but we're making progress. Although, I'm sure this murder investigation will hold us back. Reporters are swarming that field."

Bart and Anna arrive back at their little house before Detective Miller calls. "Anna, that guy had a wallet with identification for Albert Meeks. Although, I believe he is Alvin, Maddi's dad. He was deteriorating, but the coroner said he had a red birthmark on his right hip and no scars on his hands. They've put a rush on the DNA. Don't let the children return to the Meek's home. Make up an excuse, if you have to."

The next morning, Mary takes Hank and Danny to school, but the younger children stay with Anna. Before noon, large ruffled snowflakes float to the ground like feathers. Anna makes chili and grilled cheese sandwiches and lets the kids eat in the sunroom so they can watch the snow.

Bill giggles and whispers to Curt, "We may get to miss school for the rest of the week."

Anna sits them in a circle and listens to them read. Curt can only identify a few words in Carol's picture books, but he is eager to learn. She suspects that Maddi may have a photographic memory—she never has to repeat a word for her. After they read for an hour, she puts on a movie and gives instructions that no one is to make a sound or look out the front window if anyone comes to the door. They nod in agreement, and Anna spreads her books across the sunroom table.

Maddi and Carol, followed by the boys, come to ask if they can bake cookies.

"How does oatmeal raisin with pecans and coconut sound?"

"Yeah." They giggle and slap hands.

While the cookies bake, Anna mixes cornbread muffins and makes a large chef salad. Hank and Danny gobble more chili, muffins, and cookies before going to feed the horses and Curly. Then, they rush to the basement to do homework and practice their music.

The news media is busy with traffic problems caused by the snowstorm, and barely mentions the man found in the ravine.

Mary announces, "Children, in this cold weather, you will not be going to the Meeks' house to swim. Hank and Danny must go outside to feed the animals, but I want the rest of you to stay inside at all times."

Carol asks, "Can't we play in the snow with our sleds?"

"No. Not this time. Many people have the flu. I don't want to take any chances on you getting chilled and sick."

Carol frowns. The other children turn their eyes toward the sunroom window.

Later, when Anna is alone in the sunroom, Hank asks with a low whisper, "Have you heard anything from Detective Miller?"

"The guy had a wallet on him with Maddi's uncle's identification. I don't think she knows that she has an uncle, so don't say anything about it to her or the other kids."

Hank nods.

By week's end, the police determine that the Mr. Meeks, living down the street, is Maddi's uncle. Ling is his wife. They have not found evidence that Maddi's dad ever married. The twin brother took over his brother's identity, his home and his job without anyone asking questions.

Detective Miller stops by the Dugan home on Friday

afternoon. Mary and the professor drive into the garage as he rings the bell. Anna has prepared salad, spaghetti, and meatballs, with apple cobbler for desert. The table is set and hot garlic bread toasts in the oven. Going to the oven for the bread, she calls, "Everyone, take a seat; dinner is ready. You too, Doug."

The detective stares at the brimming bowls and the steaming cobbler on the stove. "Heck, I can't resist this kind of temptation." He takes a chair next to Hank and bows his head for the prayer.

Anna can hardly wait until the children go into the den to watch a movie. She has many questions and worries to discuss with Doug Miller. At last, Hank starts the movie and gets the younger children settled.

Gently, Hank closes the door to the den and returns to the sunroom. "I'm as anxious as anyone to hear about the investigation. Danny and I won't mention it to the little kids, but Danny and I don't keep secrets from each other." He sits at the table next to Bart.

Doug takes a sip of coffee and clears his throat. "I don't have the news that I wanted to bring you. We have not found Granny, and we don't know who killed that man and woman, but we believe the motive was jewels and the Meeks' fortune. Ling is one suspect. You can see her seethe with jealousy when anyone talks about Maddi's mama. Evidently, both twins were fascinated with Twila's beauty—Ling is very intelligent but far from beautiful."

Hank takes a glass of punch from Anna and rests it on a coaster. "I didn't see any blood on either of the bodies. Have you discovered what killed them?"

"Yes; it was antifreeze. She had a lot of bruises from a beating, but antifreeze killed her."

"Antifreeze?"

"It was probably mixed with vodka, but antifreeze killed them both. Ling is in custody now. Other investigators are talking to her and trying to get a confession. We still have a lot of unanswered questions. Where it was purchased is one. That sold in the US today is easily detectable in food or drink, but the killer may have bought it outside the country or had an old container bought before the new regulations went into effect."

Mary stands and reaches for the coffee pot. "Soon, I'll have to tell Maddi about her dad. It's too bad she didn't get to meet him."

Doug holds his cup for a refill. "It is sad, but she's in line to inherit a fortune. That company where her dad was working is part of the Meeks' estate. If her uncle is found guilty of murder, it may all belong to Maddi—unless another crazy relative tries to steal it by killing her."

Anna's hand trembles as she takes a sip of Bart's hot chocolate. "Isn't it ironic that a little girl with barely enough to eat a few months ago is in line to inherit a millionaire's estate?"

"It is, but if that greedy grandma is still alive, she'll be working to take it from Maddi. We have to find that woman." Doug nods toward Hank. "You boys keep an eye on those buzzards. When the weather turns warm again, they may start circling another area."

Bart looks at his watch. "I want to get an early start tomorrow. While snow is still on the ground, I want to burn those brush piles. Hank, do you think you and Danny can help?"

"Sure; we were wondering what we could do tomorrow. We're getting restless from staying inside so much this week. I just hope we don't find any more dead bodies."

Detective Miller laughs. "I don't think you will. I bet Granny is hiding somewhere waiting for Maddi to inherit a fortune."

Chapter Eighteen

Anna rolls out of bed when her alarm rings at six and runs to switch on the Amish heater in the kitchen. She adds kindling, a wax fire starter and some small dry sticks of oak to the wood heater before clicking the lighter under a crumpled sheet of newspaper. The kindling cracks, pops and releases a delicate scent of pine. Shivering, she clomps back to the kitchen in a pair of old house slippers. She could have played a soft, sissy wife and still be under the warm covers, but she knows Bart has a hard day ahead of him. He needs a good breakfast and a warm start to his day.

She has bacon, eggs, biscuits, gravy, and a pot of coffee—hot and ready when Hank and Danny knock on the door. Bart comes into the kitchen with shoes untied, struggling to pull a sweatshirt over his head and two thick undershirts. "Good morning, boys. Eat a good breakfast. We have a busy day ahead. I want to set those ditches on fire and cut down scrub trees that were too big for the brush hog. It will take us years to get them all, but we can make a dent. By the time you boys are ready to build homes, I hope this area looks like a park."

Anna hands them each a plate. "Help yourselves. I wish I could help with the brush, but I have to clean the Dugan house and watch the younger kids. I would love to be outside, even in the cold. If the temperature gets warmer this afternoon, Mary might let me take the kids to clean that sandy area near the creek."

Bart frowns at her. "I know you want to get outside, but I'm afraid for you to bring them into the woods until the police catch that murderer. Whoever did that could be a serial killer and live in this area."

She shakes her head. "I don't think so. I believe Ling planned it, but that boyfriend did the killing. He's out on bail, but the police are watching him."

Bart finishes his egg and bends to tie his shoes. "Hon, if you do take the kids out, wear your gun, and keep it loaded."

"I doubt it will get warm enough, but I'll be careful. You guys do the same." She stands on tiptoe to kiss Bart and slaps hands with Hank and Danny.

Before washing the dishes, Anna watches Bart and the boys walk toward the barn. After making the bed, she locks the house and goes to the Dugan home. Mary is eating cereal, Carol is stuffing frozen waffles in the toaster, Maddi dabs butter and a spoon of jam on top when they pop up. Bill and Curt eat them as fast as possible.

Professor Dugan comes downstairs wearing a pair of stained coveralls. Mary grins at him. "What awful job do you have planned for today that calls for such a classy outfit?"

"I'll help Bart, Hank and Danny cut, pile and burn brush. Fence building will have to wait until this snow is gone."

"Well, promise me you won't stay outside and get too cold or overtired. I have grocery shopping to do. I should be home before lunch."

Anna waits until Professor Dugan takes a bite of waffle before speaking. "Mary, if it warms to around fifty degrees, do you mind if I take the four younger kids to the creek? I would like to clean off that sandy area. Now, while it's too cold for snakes to crawl, is the best time to clean it, and it's a good time to burn the brush."

"Make sure they all wear hats, gloves and old clothes." Mary leaves for the market. Professor Dugan heads for his truck with a thermos of coffee.

Anna yells, "Kids do you want to help me clean off a beach next to the creek?"

"Yes!" They chime.

"Then first we have to clean this house. Boys, go to your rooms and collect your sheets, towels, and dirty clothes; get Hank and Danny's too. Girls, do the same in your rooms. Carol, get your mom and dad's."

Anna cleans the stove, kitchen, and bathrooms, and gives clean sheets to the children to put on their beds and helps each one straighten his or her sheets, blankets, and bedspread. She starts the washer and gives clean towels to each child to hang in the bathrooms. They all dust, vacuum and clean until Anna is satisfied with the results.

While the last load of clothes wash, Anna makes a pot of vegetable and tortilla soup for lunch and two batches of no-bake cookies.

"Wow. I love this kind of cookie." Maddi shouts. "My friend at the restaurant used to make them once a week. She always saved some for me."

"While the cookies cool, I want to teach you girls how to fold sheets."

They shrug. "Okay. That can't be too bad."

They wad the fitted sheets more than fold, but they do a good job with flat sheets.

Anna serves the children bowls of soup. "You can each have three cookies when your soup bowl is empty. "Bill, it's your turn to say the prayer. I have to vacuum Mary and the professor's bedroom while you eat."

Bill stands to stare at her. "I've never said the food prayer before. I don't know how."

"Today is a good time to learn. Place your hands on your legs and fold under a finger for the most important things to pray for at mealtime. First, thank God for all our blessings and fold under a finger. Ask God to bless this food and fold under the second finger, and to help it nourish our bodies and then fold under the third finger. Thank him for sending Jesus to save our souls and fold under the fourth finger. Say in Jesus name we ask these things; fold under your thumb and say Amen."

He takes a deep breath and starts his prayer. "That wasn't so hard."

"Of course not, and you can add as many blessings as you want to your prayer. After the first four you don't have to count."

She goes upstairs to vacuum. The girls put away the last load of clothes while the boys load the dishwasher. "What wonderful helpers you are. Now you can go change into some old clothes, and find hats and gloves."

Anna finishes sweeping and mopping before the children come downstairs. "We've finished this job, but Mary's here with groceries. We'll help her put those away and then rest for an hour before going to the creek." Bart, Professor Dugan, Hank, and Danny come in for lunch while the younger children rest.

Professor Dugan plops into a chair. "We have to hurry; the brush is still burning in the ditches. I don't like to leave it for long."

Mary and Anna serve bowls of soup, extra tortilla chips and pour fruit punch into iced glasses. Anna sets a platter of cookies on the table before going to change into warm work clothes.

She comes downstairs in insulated coveralls with a red bandanna tied around her hair.

Bart winks at her. "You remind me of Rosie the Riveter."

She returns the wink and raises a fist. "Don't get in the way of an American woman."

"But where is your gun?"

"I've got it. These coveralls have zippered pockets."

Anna piles rakes, hoes, a shovel, and a small chainsaw into the bed of Bart's truck.

Bart lifts the saw. "Kids, I don't want any of you to touch this chainsaw. Anna, I don't like the idea of you using it either. Chainsaws, even a small one, can kick back and cut you. Let me take this and I'll come down and get the brush you want cut."

"Dad taught me how to use it. I'm careful."

He pauses with it in his hand, shakes his head and puts the saw in the truck.

At the creek, Bart takes the chainsaw and cuts briars and brush from around the sandy area. The children remove the other tools before tossing brush into the truck bed. They rake all the small debris into a pile in the center of the clearing. Anna strikes a match to set it on fire. The damp brush and leaves burn slow and reluctant until nothing but a few embers and charred acorns are left. The children rake sand over the glowing remains.

Anna looks around at the clearing. "Now we can come here for picnics and maybe to swim, but that depends on what spring rains do to the creek and its banks. We'll probably have to do this again before summer." A limb from a large oak hangs over the water, other limbs tower high above, and blackberry briars climb the hill near the creek. Wild grape vines circle and hang from a tree farther down the stream's side.

"I wish Bart had left my chainsaw. I want to cut all those briars. Blackberries attract rodents and insects. Rodents and insects attract snakes. I don't want those critters hanging around."

Bill takes a hoe and walks toward the hill. "Anna, there's a cave in that hill. Can we explore it?"

"No, it might be an animal's den." She motions for him to come back.

"What kind of animal?"

"Bear, mountain lion, wolf, or coyote. We don't want to take a chance on bothering a wild animal unless Bart and Hank are here with their guns."

"Okay." Reluctantly he walks away.

"I think we need to take our tools and walk over to where Bart and Hank are burning brush. My pistol would not help much if an angry bear roared out of that cave."

Tools in hand they walk through the melting snow. They have not gone far when Maddi stops to examine something. "Maddi, what did you find?" Anna asks.

"A button from Granny's jacket."

"Let me see. Are you sure this is from her jacket?"

"I know it is unless someone has a jacket exactly like hers."

"Can you put it deep in your pocket, so you don't drop it?"

"I don't want it."

"Give it to me. I think it's pretty." Anna takes the button and pushes it deep into a pocket. "I collect old buttons."

Bart asks Professor Dugan if he will drive Anna and the four youngest children back to the house. "It's colder now, and the wind's getting stronger. They need to be inside. We're almost finished. There's no need for you to come back." He turns to Hank. "If you'll push some dirt into this ditch with your tractor, we'll all go to the house. Danny, why don't you go on? You look cold. Hank should be there by the time you get showered and dressed."

Danny nods and turns toward Professor Dugan's truck.

"I'll wait and ride with these guys. See you kids at supper." Anna climbs into Bart's truck. "Carol, will you and Maddi take that Mexican casserole from the refrigerator and put it in the cold oven? Be sure to take the plastic wrap off the dish and set the oven at 350 degrees."

Carol giggles. "Don't you like Mexican flavored plastic?"

Anna winks at her. "It's not one of my favorites."

Anna punches the number for Detective Miller into her cell phone. "Doug, this is Anna. Can you bring another detective and come to the field where you found the last body? Bart and Hank are out here burning brush. The other kids and I have been cleaning off a little beach near the creek. Maddi found a button that she said was from her granny's jacket, and I found a thread hanging on a bush that matched one clinging to that button. There is a cave on the hill behind where I found the thread. I wish you would check it and make sure someone hasn't been using it."

"We're on our way."

Bart calls, "Anna, there is a long log chain in the truck bed. Wrap one end around the truck's trailer hitch and hook it. Now, start the truck and keep it running. When Hank gets near the ditch, I'll hook the other end to the tractor, just in case he should start sliding on this snow-covered ground. If I yell, move the truck forward."

She does as told, but Hank maneuvers the tractor close to the ditch, pushing snow and dirt over the edge without a problem. Already, the brush has stopped flaming in the other ditches.

Two police cars arrive as Hank drives the tractor toward the barn. It does not take him long to park it inside and jog back to the truck. Anna leads the way to the cave but waits on the small section of cleared beach. The officers rush up the hill, draw their guns and click on flashlights before ducking their heads to enter the cave."

Seconds later, they are outside gagging, with handkerchiefs over their noses. Anna knows that means a decomposing body is inside the cave. Bart, Anna, and Hank return to the Dugan house leaving the officers to their work.

Chapter Nineteen

Hank, visibly upset about the results at the cave, leaves Bart's truck and heads for the basement. He stops after a few steps. "Anna, I don't want any supper, but will you ask Danny to bring me a glass of lemonade or a Coke when he comes down?"

"Sure, Hank. Do you need medicine for an upset stomach?"

"No, thanks. I'm just tired. I want to get a shower and rest on my bed."

"Okay, but call my cell if you get sick, especially if you have a fever."

The kids are in the den watching a movie when Anna goes inside. Mary is in the kitchen mashing potatoes. "I've made a meat and potato dinner. I figured you would all be starving after working outside."

Anna whispers to Mary and Professor Dugan about the cave and the button from Granny's jacket. "I'm sure Detective Miller will call with information about the body. We didn't stick around for them to bring it out."

Mary shakes her head. "We won't mention it to Maddi until we have all the details."

"Hank said he didn't want supper, only some lemonade or a cola and a shower. I think the idea of what was inside that cave made him sick."

"I hope he's not coming down with that flu."

"He may be troubled because of Maddi's grandma. He's been very considerate of her since Ling upset her."

"He's kind to all the children. I've never met a nicer boy."

Professor Dugan adds, "Or one that will work like Hank. He never complains, never talks back and does more than a man's share and Danny is right beside him, doing all that he can."

Detective Miller calls while Anna is moving the vegetables from the counter to the sunroom table. Mary answers the phone and motions for Anna and Professor Dugan to follow her outside. She clicks on the speaker: "Mary, I promised Anna that I would call, so will you tell her that the body inside the cave was a big dog."

"Is that all they found?"

"We found a piece of navy blue cloth from a garment, but that is all. Someone shot that dog. It may have attacked a woman out for a walk—one with a gun in her pocket. We'll check that scrap of cloth and run a DNA test if we find any human hair. If you hear of anyone in the neighborhood that is missing a big dog, let us know. Tell Anna thanks for the call."

"A dog! Why didn't they tell us that in the field instead of letting us worry?" Anna puts on her jacket, takes a cola from the fridge and grabs a tube of soda crackers from the cabinet. "I don't want to make Danny miss the last of his movie. I'll take these to Hank and let him know that it was a dog—not Maddi's granny."

The professor reaches for the cola and crackers. "I'll take them and explain. He may have just stepped out of the shower. He'll not be expecting a girl to enter boy territory. I would rather you help Mary with dinner. I'm starved."

Anna calls after him. "See if he seems to have a fever."

Mary, stirring a pan of gravy, glances at Anna. "I'm glad it was an animal in the cave, but where is that old woman? She could be in the woods, hurt badly from a dog attack."

"She's not dead yet if she's there. Buzzards would have been flying over. I saw a couple fly close to that cave in the late afternoon. I knew something inside was dead."

"I'll call Doug and ask if the police can check those fields and wooded areas." Mary steps outside with the phone while Anna sets the table.

Stepping inside, she shivers. "He said they are checking with bloodhounds but have found nothing. The hounds keep coming back to a spot beside the road. He thinks she got into a vehicle and left, but after several days and that snow, it is harder for the dogs to hold the scent. Although, if she were still in the area, I believe they would have found her."

"I agree." Anna sighs. "Someone took her away. I wish they could run those bloodhounds through the Meeks' house."

Hank comes to the kitchen with Professor Dugan. "Anna, thanks for sending that Coke; that and a hot shower made me feel better. Now I'm hungry."

When the dishes are in the dishwasher, Bart goes to the basement to take a shower before leaving for their little house.

Anna asks, "Mary, do you mind if I shower upstairs? Our bath has hot water, but the house will be like a refrigerator."

"Of course, I don't mind. I'll loan you a robe and nightgown, so you can jump into bed when you get home."

Anna pauses outside to look across the property. Bright moonlight reflecting off the remaining snow makes the night seem like day. Ribbons of smoke curl upward from the brush piles and the scent of burning pine lingers.

"Bart, that little beach we cleaned off will be nice next summer. The creek is wider there and deep enough for the kids to swim. It might be over Curt's head, but I doubt it the way he's growing. He hasn't said a word about Ling. I thought he would ask questions."

"He probably thinks they're not going because Maddi got upset about Ling holding her underwater."

"That's reasonable. I can't blame Maddi for that. Did you know that Mary never got an answer to her inquiry about Ling's references? No one returned her phone call or replied to her letter."

"Ling probably lied, thinking no one would check."

They turn and walk in the direction of the house. Anna looks toward the creek as he unlocks the door. "Bart can we remove more rocks from that pool when the weather gets warm?"

"Maybe. We'll have to be careful of water moccasins."

"Bill said he and Hank used to swim there and that the bottom is flat rock, but every spring the rain washes in lots of loose rock and gravel. He said they always clean it as soon as it warms enough to stay in the water ten minutes without freezing."

"Then we'll clean the pool and cut all those briars above it. This will be a beautiful place after we finish our work."

"It's beautiful now. I love it here."

They step inside, Bart locks the door behind them and wraps his arms around her. "Our home is wonderful, and so is my beautiful wife."

* * * * *

Sunlight filters through bedroom curtains. Anna opens her

eyes to see Bart smiling at her. "It's a beautiful Sunday morning."

"Yes, but it's cold." She pulls the blanket to her neck.

"I have a warm fire burning in the wood stove and a pot of coffee ready."

"But it's cold between here and the fire."

He pulls a blanket from the bed, wraps it around her and carries her to the rocking chair beside the stove. "Sit still while I bring your slippers and coffee."

"This is a nice fire. You must have got up early to get it warm in here."

"I did, and I baked a can of cinnamon rolls and fried a package of sausage links."

"Wow. Breakfast is great."

They sit beside the stove sipping coffee and eating cinnamon rolls. "A procession of police cars passed here this morning—back and forth. I don't know if they found something more or if they are only trying to be thorough."

"Hand me my phone and I'll call Doug Miller."

"Do you think you should? I'm afraid he'll get tired of our questions."

"Maybe so, but I have to know." She pushes the speaker button so Bart can hear.

"We haven't found anything new." His voice sounds weary. "That old woman is not in the area and Ling is as tough as a railroad spike. She will not say a thing. Neither will Meeks, but I'm pretty sure he didn't kill his brother. Misery washed over him like rain when he heard his twin was dead. I'll call you this afternoon if we find anything. Go on to church and keep this to yourselves."

After lunch, Bart and Anna go home to study. The sun

shines warm melting the snow quickly. By mid-afternoon, only small patches exist in shaded drift areas.

Anna lifts her ringing cell phone. "Are you outside?" Mary asks.

"Yes, I'm sitting on the porch reading an assignment and soaking up the sunshine."

"Do you mind looking down the road occasionally? The girls begged to ride horses, and I gave in; now I'm having second thoughts. Hank and Danny are riding along on bikes, but I'm nervous about them riding without an adult. Charles is asleep, and I have a briefcase of work to finish before tomorrow."

"Sure, Mary. I can see along the road. I'll keep an eye on them."

She goes inside for her dad's rifle and props it against the door facing. She wants to be ready for any danger that might threaten the children.

Lifting her book, she continues to read. Every time Anna turns a page, she glances at the kids. They turn the horses and come toward her. Watching for a minute, wishing she could be riding, she flips another page, hears dogs barking and looks up. Four big, tan dogs run after the kids.

"Bart! Bart, get a gun." Her rifle in hand she runs across the rough yard. The dogs are closer now. Carol is in front on her young mare. Maddi is close behind on Polka. Hank and Danny follow. Pausing beside a small tree to brace the rifle, Anna aims, and fires; a large dog howls and rolls into the ditch. She aims and takes another one down. Two are on the other side, one nipping at Polka, the other at Danny's bike tire.

Crossing the road, she gets a glimpse of Bart behind her. Again, she stops and fires. A third dog squeals and limps into the brush. Danny looks back as the fourth dog bites at his tire. Losing his balance, he falls.

Bart rushes past Anna and hits the dog with his gunstock. Hank jumps off his bike, grabs a stick from beside the road, and hits the dog with one hard, swift blow to the base of the skull. It falls to the ground, twitching, but unable to stand. Anna shoots it before it can recover.

Bart leans over to look at Danny's leg. Feeling as if she might faint, Anna turns toward the house. Carol and Maddi stop in Bart and Anna's yard.

Carol lifts Anna's cell from a chair and calls Mary, almost yelling into the phone. "Mama, call the police. Big dogs chased us. Anna, Bart, and Hank killed some. I think one bit Danny. He's on the ground. One bit Polka. Her leg is bleeding, and she's limping."

Anna drops into a chair and leans her head against the wall. Carol holds the phone, but Anna does not take it. She is still leaning against the wall, with Maddi washing her face when the police arrive. An officer walks into the brush after the dog that escaped. Soon another gunshot echoes across the hills.

Detective Miller stops in front of the house. "Anna, those dogs are the same breed as that dead one we found yesterday. Someone around here is raising them, and they are not pets. These were trained killers. If more are near, we have to find them."

She wipes her face with the cloth Carol brought to her. "Yes, if there are more, you have to find them. I shudder to think what would have happened if I hadn't been here with my gun."

"The chief has two canine officers with tracking dogs on the way to investigate. I'll let you know what they find." He returns to the group of officers waiting on the road.

Danny did not receive a dog bite. His leather boot was scratched, almost pulled off his foot, and his ankle is sore from the dog wrenching the boot. He hit his left elbow on the street when he fell. It is swelling and painful. Mary helps him into her car and leaves for the emergency room. The younger children will stay with Bart and Anna until she returns.

Professor Dugan calls a veterinarian to check Polka's leg. Hank leads the limping mare across the field to the Dugans' stable.

Anna goes inside with the children and sits listening as the girls repeat the story of the dog attack. Again, Bill tells about the times bears chased him. "Why don't you kids make cookies? I am still weak from getting scared. That adrenalin rush must have taken all the sugar from my blood. I think a handful of cookies would do me good."

"Yeah!" They shout. Carol takes a mixing bowl from the cabinet. Maddi finds two cookie sheets, gives the boys a small can of vegetable shortening and tells them to rub it over the inside of the pans. It is not long until the first batch comes from the oven. Anna and the children fill their mouths with the warm treats. Yum-m they sigh as chocolate chips melt.

"Carol, please don't eat more than a couple. Mary doesn't want you eating a lot of sugar treats between meals. I should have given you fruit snacks, but I was craving cookies."

Maddi asks, "Can we take some to Bart and the policemen?"

"Yes, but don't give any to the police dogs," Anna says, mumbling after another bite. "Chocolate is poison to dogs."

Maddi's eyes open wide. "I didn't know that. Once I fed Curly a chocolate cookie."

Anna pats her back. "She survived, but the chocolate gives them diarrhea. Those police dogs need to work hard to find killers. We don't want them to get sick."

Chapter Twenty

The sun slips behind the hills, leaving traces of red in the western sky. A cold wind blows from the north causing Anna to pull her jacket hood tight around her face. She watches officers waving flashlights and hears others yell for the police dogs to jump in the truck. Safely inside cages, the animals whimper, waiting for a treat.

Detective Miller shows disappointment while telling Anna about the tracking dogs. "They trailed to a wooded area where a pickup truck left deep tracks beside a dirt road. I hoped we could find where those dogs lived. Even if all the dogs are dead, we need to find the owners. People like that will raise more. They're training them to kill, probably to guard a drug operation."

"We've been afraid to let the children outside until you find those killers. Today was an exception, and now we have killer dogs. Do you think Jaeger's drug ring is still after me?"

He ignores her or does not hear her question; he turns to the window. "Have you heard from Mary about Danny?"

"Mary brought him home. His ankle has a strained muscle from that dog wrenching his boot, and he has a badly bruised elbow. The doctor told him to keep his arm in a sling for a week and then go to his primary doctor. He had on a thick coat when he fell. That probably protected the bone."

"What about your horse?"

"The vet said she'll be fine if we keep her leg clean and dry. The dog's teeth scraped the surface enough to draw blood but did not damage a major blood vessel, muscle, or bone. Hank will take care of her. He's good with animals."

Detective Miller stands and looks at his watch. "Karen's cooking supper for me, and I'll be late if I don't hurry. I'll talk to you tomorrow."

Anna watches him maneuver his SUV, avoiding the news media still on the road taking pictures of blood on the pavement.

Bart puts a stick of wood in the stove. "Anna, Mary asked if we were coming over for supper. I told her that we would eat a sandwich here. I have homework to finish."

She stands. "Get started on it. I'll fix us something to eat."

After supper, Anna adds wood to the stove and puts on another pot of coffee. Bart will probably study past midnight.

Opening her book, she sits in a comfortable chair near the stove. It is not long until she is nodding. Rubbing her eyes, she stands and takes a cup of black coffee to the table where Bart has spread his books. He takes it without a word and continues writing a formula on a white legal pad. She is not offended that he does not speak and interrupt his train of thought.

Finishing her chapter, she goes to bed but wakes several times in the night thinking she has heard scratching on the porch. The alarm buzzes once before she clicks it off. Bart can sleep while she cooks breakfast. She kindles a fire in the wood stove, turns on the burner under a coffee pot, shoves canned biscuits in the oven, and breaks eggs into a skillet while a slice of ham sizzles. Covering the eggs with a glass lid and turning off the burners, she pops the top on a small can of orange juice and quickly drinks before running to the bathroom for a shower. The counselor told her that orange juice helps to stabilize blood sugar at the start of a busy day.

"Bart, you need to shower while the bathroom is warmer with steam from my bath. Breakfast is almost ready." She sits near the stove to put on her socks and shoes. Again, she thinks she hears something scratching and, this time, a low growl. She pauses to listen but hearing nothing more, goes to check on the eggs and biscuits.

Bart, his hair wet but combed into place, sits to put on his shoes. "Anna, did you hear a dog outside last night?"

"Several times, I thought I heard scratching, and once a low growl."

"One dog may still be alive. I want us to leave at the same time this morning, and I think we should have guns."

"I'm gonna call the police department and ask them to send someone to check." Leaving dirty dishes in the sink, she goes to comb her hair, collect books into a backpack, and call the police.

"Ms. Grayson, it will be a while before we can get over there. We have several traffic problems this morning. An officer will be there as soon as possible."

Thanking the dispatcher, she closes the phone, slips into her coat and backpack, and buckles the holster around her waist. "Bart, I'm taking my rifle. If one of those dogs or a bear is outside, I want something to stop it. That pistol might only injure a large animal."

"I've got too many books to carry a gun. You'll have to shoot for us both."

"I'll do my best." She glances at the clock. "We have to hurry. You can't be late."

He closes the vent and stove damper, takes his books, gives

her a kiss, opens the door and turns the lock. They ease onto the porch, looking right and left, Anna has her rifle ready for anything. Not seeing an animal, Bart gets into his truck and starts the motor.

Anna places the rifle in her car's trunk but does not take the time to remove her backpack before backing from the garage. Bart closes the garage door, taps his horn and drives away.

Stopping at the edge of the road, she steps from the car, ready to slide out of her backpack. With hands at her sides, she jiggles the pack to slide it off her shoulders. One arm is out when an animal pounces on the pack and knocks her to the ground. Anna pulls herself under the car. The backpack, still looped over one arm, is too wide to slide underneath. She does not dare stretch out her arm to release the pack but holds on with both hands to something under the car.

The animal yanks and shakes the backpack. Its strength is so strong that she cannot turn loose of whatever she grips to reach for her pistol—afraid the animal will pull her from underneath the car. "Lord, help me!" Anna prays.

Abruptly, the animal stops tugging on the pack, barks and jumps inside the car. Turning loose, she slides the strap off her arm, pushes the bag toward the rear of the car so the door will not hit it, grabs the door and slams it.

The dog, trapped inside, jumps about growling and bouncing the small vehicle. Anna reaches into her pocket for the keys and pushes the button to lock the doors.

Removing her cell from the backpack, she calls 911. It does not take long for a police car to arrive. The large dog has ripped seats with his teeth and drooled from front to back.

A rookie officer stands bewildered. "If I open the door he'll jump out—maybe run away, or attack before I can shoot."

Anna looks around for something strong enough to break a window. Bart left an axe standing beside the house after he sharpened it. She runs to get it. "Officer, I'm afraid to try and hit that tiny window with an axe. But I'll hold this blade against that little side window if you will hit the other side with a stick of that wood."

"You want to break the window?"

"Yes. He can't get out that little window. All he can do is poke his nose through, but you can shoot him. Hit the blade hard."

"He'll get blood all over the inside of your car."

"It's already ruined. I want him killed."

The dog lunges at the glass, growling and showing his teeth.

"I don't know about this."

Anna yells, "Hit the axe and keep hitting it until the window breaks, then shoot the monster."

"Okay." He hits the axe three times before the window breaks. Quickly, drawing his gun he shoots the dog. It whines and slumps onto the seat.

"Shoot it again—it's not dead."

He aims through the broken window and pulls the trigger.

The dog lies still. "Can you drag him out of my car?"

The young officer puts on a glove, grabs the dog by the back of the neck and pulls. It plops onto the ground and whines—he shoots it again.

Mary worried because Anna did not arrive to take the children to school, stops on the road.

Hank runs to Anna. "That makes six dogs. I wonder if there are more."

"I hope not. Mary, can you take Hank and Danny to school? They don't need to be late. I have to change clothes before I go to class. I've been under the car, trying to stay away from that dog."

"Sure, I'll take them. Then, I'll come back and get the others. You might need help if your blood sugar drops again."

Anna grabs Hank's arm. "Thank you again for that jerky. It was the best present I've ever received."

Hank squints, staring at her. "What do you mean?"

She grins and impulsively hugs him. "It saved my life. That's why the dog jumped inside my car. Beef jerky was on the dash."

"Oh, that bag of good jerky was wasted on that awful dog."

"Not wasted, bro. It saved me." She reaches toward the girls. "You and Bill need to get inside. I don't want to take a chance on another dog being out here."

Detective Miller arrives while Anna is on the phone with her insurance agent. "Get your books. I'll take you to school as soon as Mary comes to get the other kids."

Anna looks at her torn backpack. "I wonder if the teacher will believe a dog ate my homework."

"Anna, what kind of dogs were those mean ones?" Carol asks.

"Detective Miller thinks they are pit bull terriers. Those we shot were trained to kill. I don't want you kids outside, except in the Dugans' backyard, until we find out where they came from and we know that no more are running free."

On Tuesday, Mary takes the girls to their classroom and cautions the teacher not to allow anyone other than Anna and herself to take the children from school. Things are peaceful for a few days. The snow melts away; the yard is drying, yet Hank will not permit the children to ride Polka. "When her leg is completely healed, you can ride her."

The girls take turns riding Carol's horse while Polka neighs from her stall. Curly stands beside Polka and barks when the girls pass on Apple.

The police still have Maddi's Aunt Ling and Uncle Albert in custody. They do not have any leads on Granny.

Two weeks later, a man calls the station and reports that a family in Madison County, near White River, appears to be raising pit bull terriers. He thinks they are also growing marijuana in an old chicken house, but refuses to leave his name when questioned.

Time rocks into spring while drug enforcement officers watch the activity at the Madison County farm.

Albert and Ling Meeks await trial for the murder of Alvin Meeks. No relatives or friends come forward to visit or offer support. Maddi never mentions the Meeks or her granny.

* * * * *

Bart steps into the sunroom where the children concentrate on homework. "Kids, I want you to run down to the basement and look at what I brought for the boys. I only have two of them, so you can draw straws or do whatever you think is fair."

All six children jump and run. Anna turns off the burners under vegetables she is cooking for supper. "I want to see, too."

Bart and Anna hold hands as they follow the children to the back entrance. "What did you bring?"

"Wait and see."

"Then walk faster."

The children, except Hank, kneel to comb fingers through the fur of two bearskins.

Bart stands grinning. "My friend got an 'A' in his class and won first place in a contest for his work on these. Have you decided who gets them?"

Hank takes a step backward. "I don't want one. Danny is the oldest; he can have the big one. Bill and Curt can have the small one in their room."

"Wait a minute." Bart pauses. "A man at school wants to buy the big one. He said he'd give a thousand for it. Danny, do you want to sell it? You could buy a horse with that much."

"Wow! A thousand dollars. Hank, what do you think? Should we sell it?"

"I would, but it's not mine."

"If we had three horses and rode double, all six of us could ride. Let's sell it."

"Bill hands Danny the small skin. You can have this one if you'll let us ride your horse."

"It's a deal."

"Hold on." Bart waves a hand. "Boys, we have to finish that fence before you can get another animal."

Hank flexes the muscle in his right arm. "I've been working on it. I try to set three posts every afternoon after school. I'm building a fence and, at the same time, muscles in my arms."

Danny frowns. "I wish my arms would grow. I can barely lift the post driver."

"Spring break is coming in March." Bart puts an arm around Anna's shoulders. "We'll be out of school for a week. We can go to Anna's farm, or we can build a fence."

"Ahh." Danny groans and crams both hands into his pockets. "We can't sacrifice our vacation. We have got to go to the farm."

Anna folds her arms and stands silent. Bart shakes his head. "I'll tell you what we can do—we'll ask the professor to help and every Saturday between now and March we'll work on it. With Hank and Danny working after school, we should have it completed by spring break."

"Deal." The boys slap hands.

Anna unfolds her arms and slaps the girls on the back. "We'll have breakfast ready at dawn, every Saturday until we have a pasture fence. Are you girls willing to help?"

Carol and Maddi nod. "Sure; it's our pasture too."

Saturday morning, at five-thirty, Anna starts cooking breakfast. Hank and Danny knock at the door before Bart gets his boots on. Hank lifts a lid covering scrambled eggs. "Uncle Charles said he'll bring the girls in a few minutes." He grins and looks sideways at Anna. "I doubt it. I bet they all went back to sleep. I think we should start without them."

Danny nods in agreement. "They'll delay us an hour or two if we wait."

Anna removes covers from the pans and platters. "Grab plates and help yourselves; Bart can say the blessing when you get to the table."

The boys are in the field, and the dishes washed and put away before the professor arrives. Anna opens the door as he steps onto the porch. "Come on in. I saved you a plate. Sit and get started while I pour coffee."

Quickly, he digs a fork into the eggs. "I waited for the girls, but Mary put them to stripping beds and sorting laundry. She said she'll stay with them until you get there."

Anna glances at the clock. "I planned to do that, as soon as I finish here. I baked a ham this morning, made potato salad and baked beans. The ham and beans are in the oven; everything else is in the refrigerator. If I'm not back before you guys are ready to eat, help yourselves. Cookies for dessert are under that glass lid."

"That sounds good to me. You run along. I'll stay here and eat all morning." The professor laughs, crams the last strip of bacon into his mouth and puts on his hat.

"Professor, I'll feel better about you guys being in that field if you'll put a rifle in your truck. It's warm today; a rattler might crawl onto a rock to sun. Take the first-aid kit, too."

"I'll do that if you'll put a handful of those cookies in a bag. Watching those guys work always makes me hungry."

Grinning, she wipes her hands on her apron and grabs a zippered plastic bag. "You can eat all you want. I knew you guys would be hungry, so I made two batches last night while Bart was studying."

Chapter Twenty-one

Anna gets her car from the repair shop—looking new again. She does not complain about paying the high deductible. Every time she remembers that big dog pulling on her backpack, she shivers.

She hauls a sack of laundry to the car and shoves it into the back seat. Looking left and right, she jumps in and locks the door. *Will I ever get over being afraid?*

Mary greets Anna in the kitchen. "The girls have the first load of sheets in the washer. Now, they are dusting. Be prepared for Maddi's questions. She's asking about her granny, mother, and daddy. She doesn't seem upset, but she has some serious questions. I've been expecting them."

"So have I."

"It's typical for a child to ask several adults the same questions."

"I'll do my best to answer them."

Carol and Maddi come downstairs singing an old folk song they learned at school. Both run to hug Mary before she leaves to go grocery shopping.

Carol sits to watch Anna clean the stove. "We didn't help you cook breakfast, but we started cleaning house. Mama said that would be more help."

"That's good. I'm glad you put the sheets in to wash. Laundry takes a long time."

The washer stops wringing; the girls run to deposit the contents in the dryer and add another load to the washer. When Carol goes to get towels from the bathrooms, Maddi asks, "Anna, why do some mamas love their kids and some don't?"

"I think it has a lot to do with them learning, love. Your mother probably never had anyone to love her—I mean, truly love her. Maybe it was the same with your granny. The scientists did studies with baby monkeys raised without a loving mother. In most cases, the orphan monkeys didn't make good mothers. I don't want you to worry about it because you have Mary and me to teach you about love. I am sure that someday you will be a good mother. I can tell you have love in your heart."

"Granny was just a baby when her mama died. She lived in an orphanage and said people there were mean."

"See, no one taught her about love." Anna wraps her arms around Maddi. "This family loves you." She gives Maddi a tight hug. "Mary and the Professor love you as their child. The rest of us love you as our sister. Sisters and brothers help each other all through life."

"I love all of you, but I'm afraid someone will take me away."

"Don't worry about that. Mary and the professor told their lawyer to file papers to adopt you."

"Really— I'll be their real child?"

"That's right."

"Mama had boyfriends to love her, but Granny said I was too ugly."

"You are not ugly. That was a cruel joke your granny played. You are a beautiful little girl, but even if you were not pretty on the outside, people with love in their hearts are beautiful."

Carol comes downstairs with an armload of towels, drops them in the laundry room and sits to listen.

"I have another question," Maddi says. "What makes some animals and humans mean, like those big dogs that chased us? Some big dogs are nice, and some are mean."

Anna takes a deep breath and exhales. "A lot of that is how they were raised. A lion in the jungle has to kill other animals for food, but one nurtured in an animal park where it never has to hunt for food might never kill. Part of it is nature; instinctively most cats will catch mice even if they are not hungry. Those big dogs that chased you were probably raised in cages, kicked and beaten, starved, and taught to attack and kill."

"I hope Detective Miller and the police catch the mean people who trained those dogs."

"I hope so, too. Now, let's hurry and clean the house, and then we can go outside this afternoon while it's warm."

After the cleaning is finished, the girls leave a note for Mary and go to Anna's house. They arrive in time to warm the beans and slice the ham before Bart, the professor, and the boys come in for lunch.

Excited about the work accomplished, Hank tells Anna, "We should finish in a couple more Saturdays. Bart drives a post, and I drive the next one. Driving every other one gives our arms a little rest in between."

Bart and the professor pull chairs to the table. After Bart says the blessing, they begin while Carol and Maddi pour lemonade and iced tea.

Pausing between bites, Bart looks at the professor and asks,

"Sir, do you think it will be safe to leave the horses in the field to graze while we're away during the day? I keep thinking about those dogs."

The professor shakes his head. "I wonder if anyone else has had problems with dogs. Tomorrow afternoon, let's drive over to that farm east of here. That man has horses and cattle."

"Maybe Hank and Danny will go with you. I need to study tomorrow afternoon."

"Sure, we'll go," Hank answers.

* * * * *

It is late on Sunday afternoon before they return from the farms. Danny speaks first. "One man and his sons raised horses and had beautiful pinto ponies. He tried to sell me one. It was gentle and what he called *green broke*. He said it needs more training before he would let a kid ride it. Anna, you need to go with us before we buy a horse. You know more about them than we do."

Hank nods in agreement. "Both of those farmers had big dogs, but they were gentle. After the owners told them it was okay, they let us pet them. Bill and Curt didn't seem to care about the horses and cows; they wanted to play with the dogs. The farmers said they hadn't seen any pit bulls running loose and hoped they didn't."

* * * * *

The family is preparing for a week-long vacation at Anna's farm during spring break. Anna orders three sets of bunk beds for the children and a king size bed for the guest bedroom where she and Bart will sleep. Two sets of bunk beds go in her old bedroom for the boys. Carol and Maddi will sleep in the dining room until Bart and the boys build an extra bedroom. Mary and the professor will use the master bedroom.

Bart, Hank, and Danny go down on a Saturday, two weeks before spring break, to set the foundation for the new bedroom, and to order concrete for a slab floor. The children have bags packed a week in advance. Mary and Anna prepare food to take. Bart and the professor order trusses and a load of lumber for delivery on Monday of spring break.

"Anna," Bart calls as he steps inside. "I've never seen anyone so excited about building as Danny and Hank."

"It's an adventure for them."

"They want the new room to be for the boy's. Do you mind?"

"No, I thought we would only have to move one set of bunk beds for the girls when it's finished."

"They suggested putting mattresses on the floor until the room is built and then assemble the beds."

"That's a good idea. We'll do that."

Detective Miller calls to tell Anna that the State Police raided the farm in Madison County that they were watching. "The drug enforcement guys destroyed several hundred marijuana plants, captured ten adult pit bulls and about two dozen half-starved puppies, and they rescued Maddi's granny."

"Do you know why they were holding Granny?"

"She saw them turn those vicious dogs loose near your home, and she's the one that shot the dog we found in the cave after it attacked her. Granny has a badly infected leg from a dog bite—so bad that the State Police took her to the hospital in a helicopter. Doctors want to amputate her leg, but she refuses to allow it, saying she is going to die with both legs. She asked to see Maddi, claiming she has important information for her."

Mary and Anna take Maddi to the hospital, but Granny is in such pain that the doctor will not allow a child in the room. The head nurse tells Mary, "I had a letter for little Maddi, dictated by her Granny and witnessed by one of the police officers, but the officer took the letter. In case he doesn't give it to you, I remember what she said, and will swear to it."

Maddi stands, showing no emotion, as the nurse tells Mary of Granny's condition.

Anna takes Maddi's hand. "Let's get a bag of chips and something to drink."

Maddi nods and goes with her down the hall while Mary continues talking with the nurse.

It is quite some time before they find a drink machine and even longer until they find one for chips. When they return to the floor where Granny's room is located, Mary is waiting near the nurse station. "We need to sit in the visitor's area for a while."

Maddi nibbles chips and sips a fruit punch before asking about the letter. "Aunt Mary, did that nurse tell you what Granny wanted to tell me?"

"Yes, she did. First, Granny said she wants to ask forgiveness from you, your mother, your real grandmother, and *God*. She is not your granny—she said her baby died while doctors were helping your mother and grandmother. She felt neglected and angry, so that night, she took your mother in the place of her dead baby and left the hospital in Los Angeles. She traveled to Arkansas, and has lived here since then. Your real granny was a movie star from Sweden, a beautiful blond, like your mother. Stories of the abduction were in papers across the country, but no one could track the woman they suspected because they never got her name and address when she came to the hospital. After her baby was born dead, they gave her pain medication to make her sleep and intended to get information the next day, but she slipped away during the night."

"Is my real granny still alive?"

"The police are trying to find her."

"I don't want to go with her either. Will I have to?"

Mary pulls Maddi onto her lap. "I don't know. We'll do all we can to keep you with us."

Maddi snuggles her face against Mary's collar.

Several minutes pass before Maddi sits upright with an angry frown. "That old woman was meaner than I thought. She didn't love Mama or me; she took a baby for spite—a poor little baby."

"The nurse said Granny told her that she wanted to give your mama back because the baby cried so much, but she knew that she would go to prison for taking her."

Eventually, the doctor comes out to tell Mary that Granny has died. Maddi frowns and turns to Anna. "Do you think I'll get taken away from you—to California or across the ocean to Sweden?" Her eyes widen. "I can't talk Sweden words."

"I hope she doesn't take you away. A judge will decide where you go."

Detective Miller calls to tell Mary that Maddi's real grandmother never left California after her baby vanished. Over the years, she spent a fortune on private investigators, trying to find her child. When she learns that her granddaughter is living in Arkansas, she calls the Dugan number.

Seeing the name that Detective Miller gave her, on her caller ID, Mary pushes the speaker button so Anna can hear.

"Hello, my name is Berta Wilds, Maddi's grandmother. I am eager to meet my granddaughter. Will you recommend a nearby hotel where I can make reservations or even a house that I might rent or purchase near your home? I missed a lifetime with my daughter, now I want to be part of my granddaughter's life without taking her away from a loving family."

"I'll gladly make reservations for you and look around for property. Tell me your arrival time, so I can meet you at the airport. Ms. Wilds, it will be wonderful if you have property in our neighborhood where Maddi can remain close to her adopted brothers and sister. We agonized, thinking we might lose her."

"I have no other family. Maybe I can be a grandmother to all the children."

"I'm sure they will enjoy that. What price range are you looking for in a home?"

"I was quite successful in my younger years. Money is no problem, but I want to be as close to Maddi as possible."

"I would invite you to stay in our home, but we have five children, besides Maddi. We are comfortable but have no extra rooms. The most I can offer is a folding cot in Maddi's room."

"A cot is fine. I have slept on worse while making movies, but I don't want to impose. I'll find a house or apartment."

"It's no imposition. In fact, it might be easier for Maddi if you stay here until she gets to know you."

Maddi and the other children are ecstatic with the news that the new grandmother wants to live in Fayetteville. Danny slaps hands to his face. "She'll spoil our vacation trip to the farm."

Maddi's eyes fill with tears. "You can still go, but I won't get to."

Anna frowns and bites her lip. "In the extra bedroom, we can put one set of bunk beds and a twin bed. Then, if she wants, she can go with us and sleep in the room with the girls. The boys can have the third room. Bart and I will sleep in the barn loft."

Mary shakes her head. "No, Anna. We will rent a camping trailer. It is your house. I won't hear of you sleeping in the barn."

Anna laughs. "It'll be fun. Once Mom and Dad let me have a slumber party in the barn loft. It was the best party I ever had. We told ghost stories and giggled all night. Later, Mom told me that Dad spent that night in his truck—not twenty feet away from the barn. That was probably so he could make sure Jaeger didn't sneak over to ruin our party."

Hank turns to Danny. "Let's do it. I want to sleep in the barn. Bill, will you and Curt sleep in the loft with us? It'll be a real campout."

Curt lowers his chin and frowns. "What if a bear comes along?"

"We don't have bears in that area," Anna says. "If anything bigger than a mouse enters the barn, those horses will make lots of noise. Hank will have a cell phone and can call us if you get scared."

Hank slaps Danny's shoulder. "Curt, you and Bill can sleep in the corner. Danny and I will put our sleeping bags near the ladder. I bet every boy in your class will be jealous and wish they could sleep in a barn loft."

Curt grins and shrugs. Bill nods. "We'll do it if Maddi's new grandma comes to the farm."

Mary calls Berta Wilds and explains about vacation plans to the farm. "We would love for you to go with us if you don't mind sharing a room with Maddi and Carol. Last year, we had a wonderful time fishing, riding horses, watching the stars and cooking outside. All the children are looking forward to it."

"I would love to. I have horses on my ranch here in California, and I have studied astronomy. It sounds like an excellent opportunity to get acquainted."

Mary meets Berta at the airport on Thursday afternoon and takes her home. Anna has cooked pot roast with all the trimmings. Carol made a peach cobbler, and Maddi made one with strawberries.

Berta, a beautiful blue-eyed, blond in her early fifties, laughs at every joke and shows the right amount of compassion for each story. The children love her immediately, especially Maddi.

Carol plans to spend the night with Bart and Anna so Berta can use her room and stay near Maddi, but Berta insists that she will be happy to sleep on the cot in Maddi's room. "No, Grandma," Maddi says, "You can have the bed. I like the cot."

"It's a deal if all of you will call me Berta. I love being a grandma, but I've been answering to the name *Berta* for a long time, and it's special to me."

Chapter Twenty-two

Monday morning, in the kitchen at Anna's farm, Berta states, "I see the makings of another big breakfast."

Anna laughs, "We'll work it off today. Bart, Hank, and Danny have a hard day planned, and I promised to help. Concrete for the new bedroom should be here at eight."

"I want to help, too. This family is wonderful. Everyone lends a hand. I thought I would have to die an old woman alone. Maddi's mama was my only child, and I spent years searching for her. After my husband died, I never fell in love again. Other than one cousin in Sweden, I was alone until I found Maddi and this amazing family."

Berta drops a slice of ham into a skillet. "To fill my time over the years, I've taken classes in everything from weaving to astronomy. I'm certified to teach dancing, acting and history, but a family was my greatest desire. I thank God continuously for Maddi and all of you."

"The Dugans are exceptional people. After my parents died, they took me in and treated me like a daughter. They have enough children, but we needed a grandmother."

A warm smile covers Berta's face. "I hope to excel at that job."

After breakfast, Anna and Berta cover the leftover food, leave it in the warm oven for the Dugans, and go outside with the boys.

Danny hands Berta a hoe. "Be careful and don't step in the concrete mud. It'll ruin your shoes. Hank and I have on rubber boots; we'll drag it away from the middle. You and Anna can make sure there is plenty in every corner. Stand back when the mud is dumping or it will splash all over you. Bart works anywhere he sees a problem—he's the boss; we try to do what he wants to be done."

"Thank you, Danny. I'll do my best."

Everyone works at a furious pace until the mud is in place, hardly noticing the cement truck leaving the yard and rinsing his mixer at a low place in the gravel driveway. Bart and Hank smooth and level the mud with cement boards before using long-handled trowels. Anna and Berta sit on a bench with coffee and watch Bart and Hank skillfully smooth the surface. Danny, down on his knees, goes around the outside with a trowel that rounds the edges.

Carol, Maddi, Bill and Curt ride bareback toward the creek. They did not want to wait on someone to lift saddles. Curly trots behind until he sees the neighbor's cat. A chase is on.

Curly barks, Carol yells at Curly, the horses jump and nervously dance in place. Curt, new to riding, clamps his feet into the side of the mare he rides. She jumps forward and runs toward the creek. Thoughtfully, Carol put him on Polka, the most-gentle mare.

Carol gallops Apple in front of them calling, "Polka, whoa!" The mare turns and stops.

Hearing the commotion, Anna runs to the backyard, her heart pounding, as she watches Carol take Polka's rein and lead her toward the yard. Meeting them at the gate, Anna lifts Curt to the ground.

Curt trembles, his bottom lip quivering. Anna kneels to hug him. "You're fine now. It was not your fault the animals were spooked, but it tells me you need more riding lessons. Carol has had more training, and she knew what to do. We'll get in some lessons this week. Sit on the bench with Berta until you stop shaking, and then we'll all go fishing."

Berta hugs Curt and talks softly.

Anna alternates between patting Apple and Polka as she compliments Carol. "Little sister, you did an excellent job with the horses. A teenage girl could not have done better. I lost my breath when you leaned toward Polka. I thought sure you were going to try and grab the rein while the horses were running."

Carol grins. "I thought about it, but I knew my legs weren't long enough to keep a grip on Apple and I didn't want to fall under the horses."

"You did right. For the rest of the week, get someone to put the saddles on before you go riding. The other kids need more experience, especially with that frightened cat living nearby. Let's go see what damage Curly and Fluffy did to the cement. I know they jumped in it, but I was worried about you and Curt and didn't stick around."

"You go on. I'll put the horses in the corral."

Bart and Hank are both mumbling when Anna walks near. "Hank, look at all the cat hair. I hope you boys are not allergic. These will be here forever."

"Ah, they'll be covered with carpet. Do you think I should spray some more water on this? It looks grainy."

"Probably, we'll trowel it a little more and then I think we'll have to leave it. Who would have imagined Curly chasing a crazy furball through our smooth mud?"

Hank grins. "The only way we could have prepared for that was to have locked Curly in the dog pen."

Anna looks across the field toward the neighbor's house. "Curly and Fluffy need all that cement washed off before it hardens."

Bart straightens with a groan. "Berta took care of that. She grabbed them both by the neck. Danny ran water from the hose over Curly. Berta dipped that screeching cat in the water buckets we had for washing the trowels."

"She was my cat. My neighbor promised to take care of her when I went away to school."

Bart frowns. "We weren't mean to it, but I'm aggravated that it ran through our mud."

"I know. She's an ornery old thing, but she always caught lots of mice and rats."

"That's a good thing for a farm."

Curly, locked in the dog pen, howls as the family leaves for the creek with fishing poles.

Blue-green water flows peacefully along the creek—quite a contrast from when Anna was last at the farm and floodwater filled the banks and overflowed into the meadow. She shakes her head trying to replace the vision of Bart bringing Carol's limp body from the raging stream, with one of the happy pictures stored in her mind.

Danny yells, "Anna, did you see that fish? It was a big one, teasing us to catch it."

She laughs, glad to see the children happy. "Put your hook in the water. We need several fish for supper."

Curt and Maddi have never gone fishing and have no idea what to do. Carol and Berta laugh while trying to get a fat night crawler onto Maddi's hook. Maddi, hands on her hips, watches with a frown. "That's disgusting."

Carol nods. "It is, but worth it if you catch a big fish." She tosses her hook in the water near a log and soon hooks something. "I got one. I got one."

Berta helps her pull it to the bank while Anna shows Curt how to thread a worm onto his hook without sticking his fingers. "Why can't we use those little plastic worms instead of these squishy things?"

"We'll try those another day with a rod and reel. This is only one way of catching fish."

Carol and Berta pull a big turtle onto the bank. "Don't touch it, dear." Berta cautions. "It might bite you."

Bart goes over to look. "Bite is right! That's a snapping turtle. It would bite your finger off if it got a chance. We don't want this thing in the creek where we swim." With the help of a garden hoe, brought along for digging night crawlers, he drags the turtle away from the kids.

Anna hears a pistol snap, obviously, the children did not. Danny has caught a big catfish on a piece of chicken liver. Everyone stretches to see it and guess the weight.

Curt squeals when his bobber goes underwater. With Anna's help, he lands a large perch. Anna takes a stringer from her tackle box. "Let me put it on this stringer."

He clenches fists to his chest. "Won't that hurt it? I want to keep it in a fish tank. It's my first fish."

"This won't hurt him. It will only hold him, so he can't swim away. I'll tie one end of it to this bush." After securing the stringer, she sits beside the sad looking little boy and puts her arm around him. "Curt, we can't keep these fish like goldfish.

They will only live in creek water where they can swim free. Your fish would die within a day or two if you tried to keep it in a tank."

"Then, I want to turn it loose."

"Let's think about that for a while. It is perfectly safe on the stringer. See it swimming."

"But I know it's afraid. I want to turn it loose so that it can go to its mama."

"Curt, fish are different from people and farm animals. These fish don't stay with their mama. A mama fish lays eggs in the sand or a rock crevice and goes away leaving them forever. She never returns to take care of them. If a turtle, snake or an animal doesn't eat the eggs, they hatch into little fish that swim away to nibble at grass, algae, or worms. They do not think like people, and they are not lonely or sad. All they do is swim around, find something to eat and grow, so they can be food for people or animals that catch them. God created fish to be food for people. Jesus and his brothers caught fish and ate them."

"But, Nemo—"

"Nemo is make believe. Movie artists drew pictures of fish and made the drawings into a movie. Fish can't talk; neither can real animals like in cartoons and movies. Do you understand make-believe?"

"It's pretending—not real."

"That's right. Like Carol and Maddi pretending their dolls are talking. That fish can't talk, or think any more than just trying to find food. Look, Hank caught a catfish, and Bill caught a perch like yours."

Curt runs to look at Bill's fish. "It's the same kind as mine. Do you want to put it on our stringer so that it won't swim away?"

"Sure." Bill holds his fish high, turning it from side to side. "Perch taste good. They have sharp bones, but these are big enough for Hank and Bart to fillet. With our fish, I bet we already have enough for supper. Come look at the big ones Hank and Danny caught. I used to go with Hank and catch perch from our creek. Grandma would fry them and make hushpuppy balls. This summer you can go fishing with us."

Curt plops down beside Bill and awkwardly threads a worm onto his hook. Maddi and Carol have each caught a fish. Mary, the professor, and Bart have several on a stringer before the professor declares he is hungry and thirsty. "We can come back tomorrow. We wouldn't want to catch them all in one day."

Bart and Hank clean the fish. Anna, Mary, and Berta prepare lunch. Maddi and Carol scrub their hands until they are red trying to make sure they wash away all the worm poop. Professor Dugan sits on the porch drinking iced tea and smiling as Bill and Curt practice turning cartwheels.

After lunch, Carol and Maddi push the mattresses together in their room and snuggle next to Berta for naps. The boys go to the hayloft, but Anna is still hearing shouts and laughter coming from the barn when she drifts into dreams.

Anna tiptoes to the kitchen to start beans and a berry cobbler while the others continue their naps. Berta is one step behind. "I knew you'd be in here early to start supper. What can I do to help?"

"We're having baked beans, corn on the cob and hush puppies to go with the fish. First, I'm mixing a simple-crust berry cobbler. Anything you want to do is fine with me—maybe put the corn on to boil or mix the beans."

Berta frowns. "How do you make a simple-crust cobbler?"

"Mix one cup each of flour, sugar, and milk, stir in three teaspoons of baking powder, pour it into a buttered baking dish and cover with sweetened fruit. A cake like crust will rise to the top as it bakes. I prefer a flaky pie crust, but this is fast and easy. The children love it with ice cream."

Friday night, Berta talks to the children about the planets. "I'm sure God enjoyed making his beautiful universe. I love looking at the heavens on a clear night."

Noticing that Maddi and Carol are nodding in their chairs, Anna touches their shoulders. "Come on girls; it's time for bed. She walks with the girls to the bathroom door. "Brush your teeth while I get your pajamas. Tomorrow is another busy day."

A short time later, the girls stumble back to the patio to kiss Mary, Berta, and Anna goodnight. Maddi waves to everyone and goes to the bedroom. Carol hugs her daddy and walks backward pulling on Mary's hand.

Turning to Berta, Anna says, "Carol prays with Mary. Maddi and the boys prefer to pray alone."

Despite the dim light on the patio, Berta's face shows a frown. "I notice that Mary lets you take charge of the girls, telling them what to wear and when to go to bed. I will make those decisions for Maddi when we get settled."

Anna's bottom lip drops a notch. "On school nights, they don't have to be told to get ready for bed—they know when it's time. Tonight, I watched them nodding and was afraid one might fall from her chair. Maddi has taken care of herself for so long that, once she knows the rules, she rarely needs reminding of anything."

"What I'm saying is that very soon I intend to be her only guardian."

Anna stands. "Good night, everyone. Tomorrow is a busy day—packing and unpacking when we get home." She is very tired, but Anna stares into the night, wondering if she read more into Berta's statement than was intended.

Chapter Twenty-three

Bart walks into the small kitchen and pulls Anna into his arms. "You were restless last night. Are you still upset over Berta's comment about her being in charge of Maddi?"

"I can't help it. I wasn't trying to take authority from Berta. I feel it's my job to assist Mary in every way possible. It's a labor of love. I would never try to push my ideas above what Mary or Berta want."

Bart pulls her closer and kisses her forehead. "I know. Forget it and get ready for school or you'll be late on our first day back after spring break."

"I'm not going. I only have one class this morning. One *unexcused* absence shouldn't hurt my grade. Today I want to be alone. I need time to think. I turned in my homework online."

"Hon, even in high school, you told me never to use a sick day unless I was *truly* sick. This is not like you. I'm afraid you'll regret skipping class."

She moves away to rinse her plate. "Don't give me a bad time. I need a day to think."

"Do you want me to stay with you?"

"No. You can't miss class. After I take the girls to school, I plan to saddle Polka and ride through the woods. Maybe, I'll shed some tears. Maybe I'll scream, but I need to be alone. Don't take it personal. I love you, and I'll love you even more if you can understand this." Her eyes brim with repressed tears.

"I understand, but I'll worry about you. What if a snake bites you; they're crawling onto rocks to sun on these warm days. More bears could be in those woods or a cougar, you might fall, lots of things could happen—I don't like the idea of you being out there alone."

"I'll take my gun and phone." Standing behind his chair, she wraps her arms around his shoulders and leans her cheek against the top of his head. "Bart, I love you more than words can express. To me, you are the most wonderful man in the world, and I love our large extended family, but I need a day away from everyone."

He stands, pulling her into a tight embrace, and kisses her with passion. "Let's both stay home."

She laughs and pushes him away. "That is not feasible. You have a test—remember. Eat your breakfast before it gets cold." She kisses his ear and whispers, "I'll take a rain check."

After leaving the children at school, Anna calls Mary and explains her plans. Before closing her phone she asks, "Do you think I'm too bossy and overstep my authority with the kids?"

"No. I'm thankful you share responsibilities. The children must respect you and Bart, as well as Charles and me. Now, they have to add Berta to the list."

"I'll try to be more careful with Maddi when her grandma is around. I think Berta resents my help and considers it as interfering."

"If you want, I'll talk to her. The relationship we have is family, not an employee."

"Whatever you think is best. I love the children and enjoy helping them, but I don't want her to think I'm trying to take her place. I'll pick the children up today, as usual, and cook dinner. See you this afternoon."

Anna saddles Polka and rides into the fields. Her red hair billows over a blue scarf tied around her neck. The hills and valleys display a splotchy carpet of spring grass; swelling buds bring a blush to drab branches, and daffodils sway in a brisk breeze, around the broken foundation where a house once stood. She pauses to wonder if, long ago, the laughter of children rang over those tumbled rocks.

Wild plum bushes scattered across the hills wave pale blossoms, making Anna think of ballerinas dancing on a gray winter stage. A tear slides down her cheek as she whispers into the wind, "The world changes so fast. Two years ago Mom and Dad were alive."

"The counselor at Mary's office said concentrate on the present, not the past." Choking back tears, she glances at the blue sky. "God, you must have made the professor and Mary with special clay—they are unique. How many couples with one beautiful little girl would add five orphans to their home? And me—they accepted me with all my problems and continue to forgive my mistakes." She swallows hard, touches one eye with the back of her hand, the other to her cotton sweater. "I'm lucky."

Turning Polka, Anna rides toward the creek, maneuvering around rocks, downed trees, and low hanging limbs. Near where she and the children cleared a small beach, clear water gurgles over rocks. A snake zigzags across the blue-green pool, his head barely above water.

She stops to look up at the cave on the hillside. Startled at the crack of a dry limb, she stares at the dark hole in the hillside. It would make the perfect den for a large animal—something she does not want to confront. She nudges Polka to move on.

From the top of a ridge, within the shade of a large pine, she looks across the valley. In an area where the creek fans wide wetting the roots of scrub vegetation, two bearded men appear to be setting small plants in the mud. After easing Polka onto the other side of the hill, Anna calls Doug Miller and tells him what she has seen.

"This land belongs to Hank and Bill. No one should be down there, but it looks to me like a fertile, well-watered place to grow something illegal. Brush and weeds will grow around it, making it hard to notice."

"We'll send someone to check, but you need to get out of that area."

"Don't worry; I'm leaving. I have a class starting within an hour."

* * * * *

The bell rings as Anna slides into her chair.

The teacher stands at the front of the room with a stack of papers in his hand. "Class, although I don't call the roll every day, I expect you to be here. I've noticed several students skipping lectures. Today, you have a pop test. You should ace it if you have perfect attendance, but there will be no chance for make-up, and it counts considerably on your grade."

With a sigh of relief, Anna takes a copy and passes the stack of papers to the next student. The test is easy and only takes twenty minutes to complete. She is shocked to learn the simple quiz will count for twenty-five percent of the semester grade. Silently, Anna prays, "Thank you, Lord, for sending me back."

After school, Carol and Maddi rush inside. "Anna we're

hungry for fried chicken, mashed potatoes, and chocolate cake. Will you cook those for dinner?"

She nods and winks. "Mary put chicken in the meat tray. Set the table for me so that I can get started. After setting the table, you can play in the backyard if you've finished homework."

Berta comes into the kitchen. "Maddi, have you finished *all* of your homework?"

"I finished it at school, so did Carol."

"All right, you can go outside and play."

Putting chicken in the frying pan, Anna does not comment.

"What can I do to help?" Berta asks.

"The girls requested mashed potatoes. If you don't mind, you can peel potatoes. Mary likes to have a green salad with the evening meal. If you rather, you can make a salad. I put a package of frozen green peas in a pan. I need to set those on the stove. I'm planning as I cook, so let me know if you have ideas."

Berta selects a knife for peeling potatoes. "I like the taste of creamed potatoes, but I rarely eat them. So much starch is not healthy."

Anna bites her lip. "You can eat green peas and salad. Oh, I need to mix the fudge cake I promised to Carol. Chocolate cake is almost a tradition with her. She wants cake or peach pie every time we have fried chicken."

Berta tosses a peeled potato into a pan, splashing water droplets onto the counter. "Maddi and all of the children are slim, but I don't know how with the diet you serve them—so much starch, sugar, and fried foods."

"Mary and I make sure they have balanced meals, and they eat a lot of fruit and whole grain snacks. Active children need some starch in their diets."

"Oh, I don't think so. Far too many overweight children live in this country."

"I agree, but these children are not overweight." She pauses to retrieve a cake pan from the cabinet. "When Maddi came to live with us, she was so thin that I worried about her." Anna turns her head to look at Berta. "She is such a good child, never complains, and Carol rarely grumbles since Maddi came to us."

Anna lifts a lid to check on the chicken. "Berta, I love these children like sisters and brothers. Mary, the professor, and I have shared the responsibilities of instruction and never had problems. I know they are the parents, and I am a helper. I would never try to usurp their authority. When I tell the children to wash their hands, or it's time for bed on a school night, I intend to help. I would never attempt to go over Mary or the professor's directive."

Berta bows her head. "I understand. I can see you love the children, and they love you."

"I'll try to avoid giving instructions to Maddi when you are around. I know you need to assert your position as her caregiver, but I will continue as always with the other children. I think they all appreciate someone looking out for their welfare—especially Maddi. Attention is one thing she needed before she came here. You will not have any trouble stepping into her life. Love is all that little girl needs to flourish. We did our best, but she and the other children need you."

"Thank you. Forgive me for snapping at you a few nights ago. Everything you do for the children shows love. They are lucky to have such a helper. Can we forget my jealous remark? I want you to continue caring for her like always. None of us can have too much love."

Title: *Dark Secrets*

- Author: Nancy Powell
- Publisher: TotalRecall Publications, Inc.
- Format:
  Hard Cover: 9781590955857
  Paperback: 9781590955864
  eBook: 9781590955253
- Number of pages:288
- Pub Date: 2013

Dark Secrets is the first book in a series based on the life of a farm girl born in 1908 when the United States was becoming a world leader, and farm families made up over half of the population. Conditions for the Negro had worsened, women rallied for the right to vote, and social change in music, dance, and fashion filtered into rural areas. This book shows prejudice faced by Negroes, Gypsies, Jews, and women of that era.

The book begins with Ollie trying to get home after receiving a head injury in an attack by two boys—the same boys that she thinks raped her friend and murdered a girl in a nearby community. She remains in a coma for five days, recalling vivid events of her first fifteen years.

Ollie is competitive and contends with schoolmates, and her older brother and sister, but is eager to help with younger siblings. With a gift for premonition and healing, her ambition is to be a nurse, but when her papa has to pay a promissory note signed for a friend, he cannot afford to send her away to school. With no money for schooling, she worries about becoming a spinster. Still, she rejects all the young men—until she meets Roy.

Title: *Angels For All*

- Author: Nancy Powell
- Publisher: TotalRecall Publications, Inc.
- Format:
  Hard Cover: 9781590955888
  Paperback: 9781590955895
  eBook: 9781590955185
- Number of pages:288
- Pub Date: 2013

Angels for All is the second book in the Ollie's Angels Series. It continues the story of a young couple in love. Ollie believes in premonitions sent by guardian angels, but has no warning of the hardships to come with drought and the Great Depression.

Roy and Ollie start married life on a sharecrop farm, striving for a better future and a place of their own. Each chapter is an episode that illustrates difficulties imposed by farm life. Almost every year, Roy goes away to other states working to earn money for the mortgage and other necessities.

Ollie stays on the farm to harvest crops and care for the children. She struggles against wild animals, foraging pigs, sickness, storms, hunger, and neighbors that prowl night and day stealing everything they can, including diapers, garden vegetables, harness, and cottonseed.

Ollie offers thanks for blessings she receives, giving credit to guardian angels for helping, but sometimes berates herself for discounting premonitions of impending danger.

Title: *<u>Listen For The Angels</u>*

- Author: Nancy Powell
- Publisher: TotalRecall Publications, Inc.
- Format:
  Hard Cover: 9781590955918
  Paperback: 9781590955925
  eBook: 9781590955291
- Number of pages:232
- Pub Date: 2014

<u>Listen for the Angels,</u> the third book in the Ollie's Angels Series, begins on the road to California where Ollie and Roy move in search of a prosperous life following struggles during the Great Depression. They work at farm labor and Ollie gets a disease that newspapers call Sleeping Sickness. Others have died from the illness, but doctors do not know the cause. Intuition tells Ollie that mosquitoes cause it—she takes a quinine tonic and recovers.

They move back to Arkansas, buy a small farm and continue the struggle of rural life. Almost every fall, Roy goes away to other states to earn money for the mortgage, to buy seed and fertilizer for the next year's crop, and to pay doctor bills.

In 1946, Roy and Ollie buy the farm of their dreams, but drought destroys the harvest. In 1950, while expecting her seventh child, Ollie, gets strep throat and loses her hearing. She is blessed with twins, but four years pass before she can afford a hearing aid to enable her to hear her babies laugh or cry.

Roy tries to borrow money to start a Grade 'A' dairy farm, but cannot get a loan. Fire destroys the pasture, corn and cotton crops, and a tornado hits the farm.

The Roy and Ollie Glenn family, 1956.

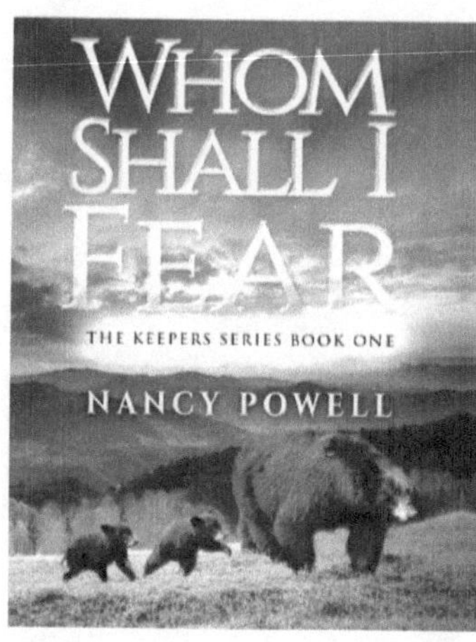

Title: *Whom Shall I Fear*

- Author: Nancy Powell
- Publisher: TotalRecall Publications, Inc.
- Format:
  Hard Cover: 9781590955024
  Paperback: 9781590955031
  eBook: 9781590955048
- Number of pages:232
- Pub Date: 2016

The Keeper Series Book One

Whom Shall I Fear is an inspirational suspense novel about a Christian girl, kidnapped and forced into an illegal marriage by a man planning to sell her in South America and collect her inheritance after she disappears.

Title: *Pursued*

- Author: Nancy Powell
- Publisher: TotalRecall Publications, Inc.
- Format:
  Hard Cover: 9781590955086
  Paperback: 9781590955093
  eBook: 9781590955109
- Number of pages:232
- Pub Date: 2016

The Keeper Series Book Three

Neglected for the first six years of her life, Maddi learned to watch for danger. Now, she has found a loving family, but someone wants her to die—her hair is burned, a landslide dumps dirt and rock on her, and she narrowly misses a rifle bullet. Someone is stalking and making her constantly afraid. At school she misbehaves so the teacher will sit her in a corner away from the windows, and at night she hides under her bed. Anna does her best to protect the children, but she still feels pursued by Jaeger's family and the human trafficking cartel.

www.ingramcontent.com/pod-product-compliance
Lightning Source LLC
Chambersburg PA
CBHW030428310726
48979CB00009B/1668/J

* 9 7 8 1 5 9 0 9 5 5 0 5 5 *